VENGEANCE

by ANDREA MURRAY

DMP

Dragon Moon Press

Copyright 2012 © Andrea Murray

Cover Design by Greg Simanson

This is a work of fiction. Names, characters, places, brands, media, and incidents are
either the product of the author's imagination or are used fictitiously. Any resemblance
to similarly named places or to persons living or deceased is unintentional.

Print ISBN 978-1-988256-12-2
EPUB ISBN 978-1-988256-13-9

Library of Congress Control Number: 2015900016

To my niece, Katie, who knows my thoughts before I do.
To Kim, who keeps me sane when I threaten to run away screaming.
To Tracie, who will always be the crazy band lady.
To Ashley, whose excitement and sweet treats make me smile.
There's a piece of each of you in this book.
Thank you

PROLOGUE

Victorious

His eyes are mine,
meeting over the table,
a look of success
as he slaps down
what he thinks is an
unbeatable hand.
Two of a kind—
like us.
Only five minutes of life separate us,
but that five minutes
trumps my desire to beat him.
I throw my winning hearts face down.
While the others congratulate him
on his first triumphant hand
all night,
his smile beams,
and he rakes the plastic chips.
It's the first smile since I told him,
told him my plans.
He doesn't understand
this desire to lead,

this need to be more than two volumes
(priceless we may be)
without bookends.
No real sense of identity,
no real family, save each other.
But he doesn't have to understand.
I will become enough for both of us.

CHAPTER ONE

HIS FULL LIPS PRESS AGAINST MINE, sweet from the chocolate he's just eaten. I inhale his warm breath and feel his heartbeat against my hand. The fast rhythm matches my own. One hand rests against my neck, fingertips brushing my hair. The other slides down my arm, caressing my wrist, before slipping to my waist and under the hem of my t-shirt. When his hand slides up my stomach, he deepens the kiss. My palm glows blue as I grip his shoulders. His teeth nip my bottom lip before his mouth slides across my jaw then down my neck. Fingertips caress my ribs.

"Vivian," his voice whispers against my ear.

I jerk upright in the seat, still breathing heavily.

"What is it? Did you have a vision?" Easton's worried expression sends a wave of guilt crashing over me. He leans close and takes my face in his hands. "Hey, you okay? Say something, babe."

I shake my head slightly. "I'm fine."

"No, you're not. You're shaking." He runs his hands up and down my arms.

"It's nothing. Just a bad dream." I try to smile, but it refuses to appear genuine. I glance across the darkened aisle of the bus where Wyck sits wadding the wrapper from a candy bar. He licks his fingertips then smiles. Even in the dim lights from passing cars, I can still see the wink he tosses me before he stretches his legs across the seat. Since the five of us are the only passengers, there is ample room on the bus, but Wyck, being his usual trouble-loving self, chose to sit directly across from Easton and me. He rests his head against the window behind him, the smile an alpha-male smirk.

Damn him! If he hadn't saved my life a week ago, I would wipe that look right off his face. But I owe him, and I've promised him my help in finding his mother. So, for now anyway, all I can do is endure his little fantasies and try to keep Easton from killing him in the process. When I'm awake, keeping him out of my head is easy. Sleeping—that's a different matter. He reminds me on a regular basis that I must enjoy our 'rendezvouses' (his word, not mine) or else he couldn't get into my head even then, and I keep trying to reassure Easton that's not true, a complete fabrication of Wyck's devious mind, but sometimes I wonder if I'm just trying to reassure myself. I have to admit if anyone is going to force dreams into my head, Wyck's are not entirely... unpleasant.

I drop my gaze but not before Easton catches the direction of my glance.

"He did it again, didn't he?" He breathes deeply, his jaw clenching from the grinding of his teeth. "That asshole!" Before I have time to react, he whips around in the seat and launches himself at Wyck.

"I warned you! I told you if you pulled that shit again I was gonna kick your ass!" Easton yells, grabbing Wyck by the front of his t-shirt and yanking him to his feet in the aisle between our seats.

"What's going on back there?" yells the driver, a tiny man with white hair and a badly wrinkled uniform.

Cooper, who's rapidly blinking the sleep from his eyes, jumps up, waking Abby who is leaning against his shoulder. In two long strides his massive body reaches Easton, grabbing Easton's arm as he pulls back his fist. "Call down, buddy. I know you're pissed, but I'm not itchin' to get kicked off this bus," Cooper drawls calmly even though he knows I would never let that happen. My powers have been weak since invading Hoyt's mind and collapsing the tunnel at the facility, but I still have enough juice to make an old man drive us to the motel. After all, I did convince the ticket lady to let us on in the first place, but in the week since we escaped Hoyt and the Liaisons, Coop's easy-going nature has been the peacekeeper. He's defused more than one situation. Easton stopped listening to my pleas after the first day.

"Yeah, 'buddy,' better listen to Coop," Wyck sneers, cocky grin back in place as though he isn't about to have close, personal knowledge of Easton's fist. "I'd hate to have to hurt you in front of our girl."

Wyck's taunt causes Easton to shake off Coop's hold and throw all his weight against Wyck, slamming him against the window.

"Stop it right now!" The driver pulls the bus to the side of the interstate.

"Easton! No!" I jump up to separate them by any means necessary, but Coop captures Easton in a bear hug and yanks them backward then swings around, putting himself between the two of them.

"Now quit it!" He's panting a little as he grabs Easton's shirt. "I know you wanna kick his ass, but it ain't happenin' right now! We've spent the last week movin' from place to place, tryin' to keep us all alive and get back to the motel where we can get our shit and get the hell away from here! We're almost there, and you and pretty boy can kill each other then! We're all worn out, so both of you sit down and don't even look at each other!"

I don't think I've ever heard Cooper say so much at one time. From the expression on his face, I'd say he's ready to beat the crap out of both of them, and they'd deserve it. It's been—as Aunt Charlotte would say—a rooster parade since we rode away in the boat we stole to escape the Liaison's facility. To his credit, Wyck hasn't once tried to use his Gift against Easton. In fact, he hasn't tried to use it at all, and I'm beginning to wonder if his ability to stop time was just a one shot deal. It sure would be nice to have Griffin's power and reverse the last thirty seconds, but Wyck's twin chose his side when he stayed with the Liaisons right after he broke his brother's heart by admitting that he knew the truth about their father's murder. He naively believes his mother is safe and refused to leave with us to find her. Wyck hasn't said it, but I know his brother's choice cut him to the core.

Easton roughly pushes Cooper's hand away and glares at Wyck who shrugs and sits down.

As the bus screeches to a stop, the driver throws it in park, turns in our direction, and points his finger. "Out! All of you get off this bus! Company policy says no fighting!" He moves to open the door, but I close my eyes and connect to his mind. After one stunned moment, his eyes glaze over, and he turns back to the steering wheel, puts the bus in gear, and gets us back on the highway. The simple task drains me, and my knees refuse to hold my weight. I'm pretty sure I would have hit the floor had the seat not been there to catch me.

"Vivian!" Wyck yells, moving quickly toward me, his arrogant expression replaced by concern.

"I'm fine," I say, holding my hand up before he reaches me.

Cooper touches Easton's shoulder as Easton squeezes past him and back to our seat. "Sorry, man."

"No, Coop, you're right. I'm sorry for letting him get to me." Easton shakes his head.

"Aw, you two gonna kiss now?" Wyck asks as he drops back down into his seat.

Cooper tightens his grip when Easton tenses. He glowers at Wyck in a way I've only seen once—right before he beat the crap out of Dillenger Wescott after the prom fiasco last year. "Don't push it, pal," Cooper says before releasing Easton, "or I might just help him."

When Easton plops down forcefully beside me, he takes my hand. "You alright?" His aqua eyes study my face, searching for signs of distress.

"I'm okay. Like Coop said, we're all tired. We need a good night's rest in an actual bed, not sitting up on a bus or in the bottom of a boat." I kiss his cheek. "Don't be upset." I nod toward Wyck and whisper close to Easton's ear. "I love *you*, and he just does that because he knows it bothers you. He doesn't really think of me that way, and it wouldn't matter if he did."

Easton squeezes my hand gently. "I don't want to lose you to him."

I kiss his lips and smile. "The only reason he acts this way is because I bruised his ego by turning him down." When I lean back against the seat and glance out at the dark landscape, Wyck's voice enters my head.

Keep tellin' yourself that, Princess, and you might believe it.

I quickly put up my mental block, and from the corner of my eye, I see his smile as he leans against the window again and closes his eyes. A small part of me hopes he's right.

CHAPTER TWO

"OMG! I CAN'T BELIEVE how great this shower feels!" Abby squeals from the cupboard-sized bathroom at the Shady Rest motel. "I never thought I'd be saying that about a place like this." She laughs, a real 'Abby' laugh, the first in so long. Since recovering from her stay in the facility's deluxe prison accommodations, she's been somber, like a light set on dim.

I move to the bed to unpack the garbage bag holding all of my stuff. We weren't real sure what would happen when we returned to the motel. We thought the manager might have had Abby's SUV towed and thrown out all of our belongings. As it turns out, only *my* belongings were thrown out. Well, not really thrown out, crammed into this oversized trash bag. Another day and all of my stuff would have been trashed. Since I paid in cash on a weekly basis and hadn't paid in over a week, my room had been cleaned out, but the two rooms Easton, Cooper, and Abby rented were on Abby's credit card, so the manager kept charging the card and hadn't touched anything. Abby's purse, Cooper's and Easton's wallets, even Coop's cell phone were all where'd they'd left them. Good thing this place is cheap, and the manager is honest. Abby insisted that I move into a room with her instead of paying for my own room.

I find my favorite black, v-neck t-shirt and holey jeans and lay them out on the bed before unpacking, refolding, and repacking all my clothes into my big duffle bag. We decided we'd spend one night here then hit the road in Abby's SUV. I tried without success to talk

Cooper and Abby into catching a plane and heading back home, but Abby said she wasn't leaving me again, and Cooper isn't about to leave Abby.

"Abby, I wish you'd reconsider going home." I lean against the bathroom door. "You've been through so much, and I know you're not back to 100 percent yet."

"V, I told you I'm not going home, so just stop already. My parents are in Europe for, like, another month or something. They won't even know I'm not around. I mean, they didn't wonder why I hadn't called them in so long! Guess my dad's over his scare and forgot all his new parenting lessons."

Her voice falters on the last part, and I know that it kills her that her parents aren't more loving or at least attentive. When I disappeared last spring, her father tightened up the reins, going so far as to buy Abby an unbelievably expensive SUV in hopes of keeping her safe, and even though she pretended as though his overactive parenting bothered her, I know in her heart she was ecstatic.

"Yeah, but Cooper really needs to get back to his grandmother. She might need him." I have a feeling my efforts won't convince her, but I have to try.

"Have you ever met his grandma?" Without waiting for my answer, she continues. "Well, I have, and let me tell you, she definitely doesn't need his help. She single-handedly raised Cooper when his parents split up and took off. She's been everywhere and done everything. Did you know she was a singer when she was younger? She performed in Las Vegas for, like, twenty years before she took in Cooper. So, no, V, Coop's grandma doesn't need him."

I smile remembering the huge grin on Cooper's face when he called his grandmother as soon as we got back. He told her we'd all been traveling in the mountains—true enough, I guess—had gotten stranded for a few days when the SUV broke down, and he didn't have a cell signal. He'd laughed, told her he didn't need her to wire any more money, and said he wouldn't be home for a while longer. His cheeks had turned a pretty shade of pink when he told her he loved her and hung up.

When Easton had spoken to his mother, I could hear the relief in her voice from two feet away. She'd cried and demanded to know where he'd been, why he hadn't called. He'd given her the same excuse Cooper had used so that their stories would match up. She'd not taken the news quite as easily as the Coop's free-spirited grandmother. She said she'd have called the police if she hadn't spoken to Cooper's grandmother, who insisted the boys were fine and called her ridiculous for overreacting—thank you, Grandma McNeal. She also wasn't pleased to hear he wasn't coming home right away.

"I'm eighteen, Mom," Easton had said, scrubbing his hand over his face. "I'm using my graduation money, and I'm not coming home right away. I promise I'll call more often." Whatever she'd said had caused Easton to throw up his hand in frustration. "Put Dad on the phone. I can't deal with you when you're like this."

Apparently, Easton's dad is a lot like Grandma McNeal because after explaining it all to him, Easton sighed and smiled, his dad having agreed with Easton.

When he hung up, I'd said, "Wow, bet your mom *loves* me for dragging her son all over creation." I shook my head and jumped up from the bed, pacing from the bed to the door. "I've screwed up everything. I emotionally damage you with my vanishing act then I almost get you all killed! Just go home to your normal life, Easton." I'd leaned my forehead against the door, willing the wood to open up and swallow me.

"Not true and not going to happen, babe." He'd put his arms around me and kissed my neck. "Okay, maybe the 'emotionally damage' part." He'd laughed and tickled my ribs until I'd squirmed free. "You are *not* getting rid of me, so stop trying."

Abby's voice brings me back to the present. "V, I need a towel."

Grabbing a towel from the rack near the door, I toss it inside. I flop back on the bed to wait my turn. I must have dozed off because when I crack open my eyes a fully-dressed and make-upped Abby is rifling through her purse on the bed beside me. Her blonde hair ripples around her face and over her purple glasses.

"Sorry, didn't mean to wake you," she says, tossing out her wallet, a comb, her broken cell phone. "Aha! I found it!" she exclaims with a huge smile as she unscrews the lid from a tube of sparkly lip gloss. "It's Cooper's favorite flavor, Creamy Coconut Confection." She smears on a shimmering glob then smacks her lips together. "Will you be okay alone? Cooper came to the door and said he'd be done in a few minutes. We're going to fill up the SUV so we'll be all ready tomorrow morning. When we get back, everyone should be ready, and we can get some food." She checks her appearance one last time when someone knocks on the door. She doesn't wait for my answer before she zooms to open it. Cooper's eyes grow big as saucers when he sees her tight, red shirt and mini skirt.

"You look... wow, sunshine... that shirt's really nice." His soft brown eyes are glued to her boobs. His hand adorably tangles his blonde locks.

She grabs him in a fierce hug, pressing her enormous assets against his chest. "I knew you'd like it. I didn't have a chance to wear it before we were—"she breaks off and turns toward me.

"Kidnapped, Abby, before you were kidnapped because of me," I finish for her.

"We're not going to discuss this for the hundredth time, okay? Shower, V. You smell." She smiles and waves her hand in front of her nose.

"Will do, and have fun." As they turn to go, I say, "Oh, and Cooper, make sure the SUV is the only thing you 'fill up' otherwise we may never get to go eat."

He chuckles. "No promises, Vivian. There's some beef jerky left in my backpack just in case." He winks and closes the door behind a giggling Abby.

I drag myself to my feet and trudge to the shower. While I shower, I think about how lucky I am to have Cooper, Abby, and Easton. When I lost Aunt Charlotte and took off in her car, I thought I'd be alone forever, and I probably should, considering how dangerous my life has become since Hoyt Matthews decided to have our little family reunion. Watching the others call home to assure the people who love them that they are fine reminded me of how alone I am, but I told Easton I would stop feeling sorry for myself, so I can't dwell on that anymore. Aunt Charlotte would definitely not want that. She'd probably tell me to suck it up and find my dad, which I intend to do as soon as I figure out where exactly to start.

When I brainjacked Hoyt, I only got a general idea of where he might be hiding before Wyck pulled me away from him and broke our mental connection. But it's more than I had before. At this point, I'm not even sure what I'll say to him or how I'll feel about finding him. I always believed I'd be happy, but I'm not sure anymore.

Hoyt's memories confirmed the information Wyck discovered in his search of the Liaison's confidential files. My father, Hoyt's twin, Harrison, seduced my mother in order to create a perfect weapon, combining her abilities with his. Only one problem. My mother refused to play nice and ran away before they could take me from her. Knowing my father was a total fake and that he didn't stop Hoyt from pursuing her doesn't give me a warm, fuzzy feeling. I only wish I'd had more time inside Hoyt's mind. The memories flooded in so fast that knowing anything for certain is impossible.

I turn off the shower and wrap towels around my hair and body. I'm so lost in my thoughts that I jump and screech at the sound of Wyck's whistle.

"Well, Princess, I gotta say that's the best outfit I've ever seen," he says from his reclining position on my bed. Leisurely sitting up like he's got all day, his indigo leer covers me from head to toe and back again.

"What the hell are you doing in here? How did you even get in?" I exclaim as my body rushes to catch my racing heart.

He dangles a room key from his finger. "This was in Cooper's room. I came to use the shower. Your boyfriend"—he sneers, turning up his lip—"is taking his sweet time, probably so that you'll leave me here when you go eat. You should've seen his face when Cooper made him loan me these." Holding up a change of clothes, he raises his brows in mocking innocence. "You know, I'm beginning to suspect he doesn't like me too well."

He glances down at my shirt and jeans spread across the foot of the bed. Realizing his intent, I move swiftly, but he's too fast, snagging them in his own hands. He saunters toward me as though I'm not practically naked, but I suppose that's exactly why he's moving so slowly, to torture me and make me feel as uncomfortable as possible.

He holds up my clothes with a disgusted expression. "I like the towels much better."

Snatching them from his hands, I hold them against me like a shield. "You're a jerk, Wyck. I'm so glad we're out in the real world now. Maybe you'll find someone else to torment." I turn for the bathroom, but he grabs my arm, forcing me to face him.

"What makes you think I don't mean everything I say?" His piercing eyes hold me.

"Wyck, don't. You're only doing this to get under my skin." When he raises his eyebrows, I quickly continue. "And to aggravate Easton."

"Who happens not to be here at the moment," he quietly murmurs.

"Wyck, what you did for me"—I shake my head—"I can never thank you enough, and I'm going to do everything I can to help you find your mom, but you and me—not going to happen."

He slides his hand down my arm, and I'm reminded of my dream. I shiver as I pull away from him. He smirks. "I'm not so sure about that, Princess."

Before he can stop me, I hurry to the bathroom and dress in record time. When I emerge, Wyck is holding the picture I brought from home of Aunt Charlotte and my mom, two smiling teenagers posing in front of a lake. He had to have gone through my bag to find it, but my anger fades when he looks up at me with his anguished eyes.

"Your aunt and mom?" At my nod, he glances back down. "It's easy to tell which is your mom. She's as beautiful as you are." He swipes at his eyes before he raises his head. "You think I'll ever see my mom again?"

I walk to him and put my hand on his back. He breathes heavily as I take the photograph from him. "I don't know, Wyck, but I'll do everything in my power to discover what happened."

"You don't have to. You've done enough already," he says, glancing away.

"I know I don't *have* to; I *want* to." I step in front of him, forcing him to look into my eyes and know that I'm as committed to the search as he is.

He runs his hand through his wavy, brown hair. "What about your father, Vivian? We don't know how long we have before they come after us. You and the others should take off before that happens, find your dad, or just get somewhere safe where they can't reach you."

I laugh humorlessly. "And where would that be? Because I want nothing more than to keep Easton, Abby, and Cooper safe. I've tried that route, and it didn't work." I smile. "Besides, do you really think they would listen anyway? You have met Abby, right? She's really good at doing whatever she wants regardless of what anyone says. And Coop… well, he's as loyal as they get." I laugh, but one look at his serious blue eyes stops me.

"I know exactly why Easton's staying. I wouldn't leave your side either." He steps in closer.

Shaking my head, I step back. "Wyck, I promise with every part of myself that I will help you find out about your mom—one way or another—but like I said, nothing but friendship can exist between us."

Undaunted, he closes the distance again. "I think it can if you'll let it." His voice sounds almost like a plea.

"Well, I won't. I love Easton. This isn't some contest between you and him, a game you can win. I'll bet a girl has never turned you down before. I think that's the only reason you're" — I grope for the right word—"pursuing me." Sidestepping him, I grab my purse and the extra room key from the bed. "I'll wait for you in Easton's room." As I step out into the darkening, twilight sky, his voice stops me.

"You're wrong, Princess. It is a contest, but I'm not just competing because you turned me down. I'm after the grand prize." Judging by his tone, his arrogance has returned. I close the door behind me and hear him mutter, "And don't expect me to play fair."

CHAPTER THREE

"YOU LOOK GREAT," Easton says, ushering me into his room. Shirt in hand, he leans toward me for a quick kiss. His muscular chest is another reminder of how unbelievably lucky I am. How could a guy like him love a girl like me? With his disheveled, black hair, hidden-lagoon eyes, and 'only in my dreams' body, he should be plastered on the cover of some cheap romance or on the red carpet for a movie premiere, screaming teenage girls grasping for a touch of his perfection. Instead, here he stands in a cheap motel in the middle of nowhere beside a freakish girlfriend with daddy issues.

"No, I don't. It's only a t-shirt and jeans," I say snappishly. His flawlessness only highlights my inadequacies, and even though it isn't his fault, I can't help feeling this way. Maybe it's Wyck's full-court press that has me so rattled. In the last couple of days, I've wondered if it would be better to be with Wyck. Though he's definitely not insecure, he has as many issues as I do. Being Gifted and chased by a psycho and his posse kind of creates a certain bond—real Hallmark moments—but at least we wouldn't be putting anybody else in harm's way. We both have a vested interest in this situation. Neither of us is collateral damage, like Easton, Abby, and Cooper are.

He pulls me against him, his smooth skin a little damp under my hand, and cocks his head. He bends so that we're eye level. "Hey, what is it? Something's wrong. Tell me."

I try to smile but only manage a sick version of one. "Nothing, everything's fine."

"Vivian, stop," he says, jostling me so that I find his gaze. "I thought we had a deal. Tell each other everything, remember? You're obviously upset. Why?"

"Easton, please go home." When he rolls his eyes at the ceiling and stands upright again, the words spill out rapidly. "I can't do this if I know you're in danger. Your parents... they sounded so upset."

He pulls away and slips on his shirt. The light blue color makes his eyes even more vivid. "Nothing you could say would ever convince me to leave you now. So give it a rest, babe. I don't give a damn what my parents want." His glib attitude ignites something inside of me. I tick off the reasons why he should leave on one hand.

"You have a home, parents who love you, and a chance at a normal life!" His shocked expression does nothing to calm my sudden resentment in his refusal to see how blessed he is. Regardless of what I told Wyck earlier, a part of me still hopes that I can convince him to leave this insanity behind and find some measure of normalcy and safety. He has what I wish I could, but he's too stubborn to appreciate it. "You can go back, start again! The Liaisons didn't bother you before you found me at the diner when you still thought I was dead. Maybe if we aren't together they'll leave you alone!"

"Didn't bother me before? They nearly killed you!" He stalks angrily to the opposite wall, as far from me as possible and swipes his hand through his tousled hair.

"Yeah, they nearly killed *me*—not *you*!" I yell, pointing at my chest.

"You don't get it do you? You aren't just some girl that I like." He sighs, shaking his head and gifting me with that lopsided, irresistible grin. "It's not a boyfriend-girlfriend thing with us. I *can't* be without you. I don't know how to explain it. From the first moment I saw you, there was something drawing me to you. I found you in this shithole town without even realizing what I was doing, and I'm going with you to find your dad." He throws up his hands, looking lost and totally kissable. "It's like a missing part of me is inside of you." He looks away, suddenly very solemn. "But maybe it's not that way for you. Maybe you can't understand why I won't leave because you don't feel the same way." He rests his hands on his head, his biceps flexed at the unfamiliar feelings of insecurity and uncertainty.

I walk toward him, wanting to reassure him. I feel the same way he does, but I don't want to risk his life to show it. "Easton, you know I do. That's exactly why I want you to leave me. I couldn't stand the thought that I was responsible for something bad happening to you." When I reach him, he won't look at me. I fist the front of his blue shirt and lean my body against his. "As much as it hurts me to say it, to even think it, maybe we can find a way to break the connection between us then you can move on."

Slowly, he turns his head. When his eyes meet mine, it's obvious he's not thought of this and doesn't appreciate the fact that I have. The hard set of his full lips, the slight flare of his nostrils—definitely not good. I've hurt him.

"I'm not saying this to upset you, but you can't tell me it wouldn't be a lot easier if you didn't need me." His expression rips at my chest like a dull knife. His aqua eyes stare into gray ones, and I wonder if mine look as pained as his at the moment.

"Easier for who?" His pain morphs abruptly into anger, his eyes now fierce at what he thinks is me slighting him for Wyck. "Is this about him? Is that it? You want to be rid of me, so you don't have to hide how you feel about him?" He clenches his jaw and grabs my wrists, loosening them from his shirt but still keeping them in his grasp between us. "Do you have feelings for him, Vivian?"

I don't know how to answer that question. Yes, I feel something for him—compassion for the loss of his dad, sorrow over his brother's decision to stay behind, kinship because we're both freaks, lust... okay, maybe a little of that, too. But do I feel for him in the same way I do for Easton? Not even close.

"He's not the one I'm willing to do anything to protect, even if that means being apart. He's my friend, Easton. Those bastards killed my mother, but there's still hope that we can save his, and without his help, none of us would have escaped," I reply in a small voice.

"We could have done it without him," he growls, his brows drawing together above his stormy eyes. I've never seen him so resentful and pissed off. Why is he being like this? Don't we have enough problems without this testosterone, caveman bullshit?

"No, we couldn't have! And I would have had to—" I stop. Despite our promise to tell each other everything, I have yet to confess the terrible deed Hoyt forced me to commit, killing the blonde swimmer the morning after we captured Zeb. Each time I've tried to tell him, my mouth and throat would seize up at the thought he might never be able to forgive me. Not being able to have Easton for his protection is one thing. Not being able to have him because he can't stand the thought of touching me, that's quite another.

"You would have had to what?" Easton asks, his face ripe with questions.

I swallow hard and gaze down to hide the sudden tears. He gives me a little shake, causing one of the tears to break free and run down my cheek.

"To do what?" he repeats, more forcefully.

"Easton, I'm not the person you think I am. You deserve more." More tears fall when I finally raise my face to his. "I've done something that—"

A resonating knock on the door echoes throughout the room.

"Hey! Let me in; it's raining out here!" Wyck's voice, muffled but clearly agitated, comes through the door.

"Go away!" Easton shouts. "We're busy!"

"I can't! I'm locked out of both rooms, so open the damn door!" he yells.

"Both rooms?" From the look on his face he must have just deduced where Wyck took a shower. "He was in your room?" His body tenses. His fists clench at his sides.

Another round of pounding echoes from the door. "Open the door! You two can make out later!" Then he mumbles, "I can't believe I just said that."

Easton touches my face tenderly, his thumb brushing away the tears. "We'll finish this discussion later. First, I need to have one with him." He stabs his finger toward the door as if he were stabbing Wyck himself.

"No, Easton, all he did was shower. We didn't even talk." I cringe at the small lie, glad that Easton can't see my face.

He jerks open the door, and a soggy Wyck glares at us both. "What took you so long? No wait, don't answer that," he says with revulsion on his face as he shakes out his shaggy chestnut hair and swipes his hands down his arms, slinging water in all directions. "I'm soaked thanks to you."

"We were just talking about why you went to Vivian's room after Cooper and Abby took off." Easton's eyes sparkle dangerously as he steps up to Wyck, and his fists clench and release at his sides.

Wyck rolls his eyes. "Oh not again! Listen, asshat, nothing happened. I showered. She left before I even got started, okay?" Wyck passes us both to retrieve a towel from the rack above the sink. I catch his eye in the mirror, and he winks.

"I saw that," Easton says, and I step close to Easton's chest, my eyes pleading for him to let it go. He makes a low grumbling noise and sighs, closing his eyes momentarily to calm himself. Grabbing his wallet from the small bedside table, he stuffs it in his back pocket forcefully. He may have let Wyck pass unscathed, but he is definitely not satisfied. Wyck chuckles behind the hand towel.

"Alright, enough from you both." I wave my hands in a sign of surrender. Seizing Easton's hand, I tug him with me across the room. After we're standing in front of Wyck, I step aside so that he and Wyck are face to face and hold up the hand I've just used to haul him over. I pick up Wyck's hand. "Shake hands."

"You must be kidding, Princess." Wyck tosses the towel onto the sink.

"I don't think so, Vivian." Easton shakes his head, never breaking eye contact with Wyck.

"We're going to be together for the foreseeable future, and we have enough to deal with without this macho, whose-junk-is-bigger crap." They both turn wide-eyed expressions on me, but I continue. "So, you are going to have to get along. Now, shake, and that is not a request."

Wyck chuckles, shrugs, and drops his hand. "Sorry, not happening, and you can't make me," he says, sounding every bit like a kindergartner refusing to take a nap. His dark blue eyes twinkle, and his roguish smile is disarming—almost. At this moment, I'm way beyond his boy-band good looks.

"Would you like me to try?" I reach up and put my right palm on his arm, hoping I have enough juice to give him a little scare. Before it even begins to glow, Wyck extends his hand to Easton, who suppressing a smirk, takes his hand in a white-knuckle grip. Wyck grimaces and grunts, but he doesn't let go until Easton does.

When they finally break the hold, both of them rub their hands to restore circulation. I put one arm around each scowling boy but neither bothers looking at me. Instead, they choose to glare holes through each other. They'll never be friends, but this is a step towards tolerating each other at least. I smile sweetly. "See, doesn't that feel nice? How about we try a hug now?"

"Don't push your luck, babe," Easton growls as he turns away.

"I'd rather you barbeque me instead," Wyck retorts.

Yep, gonna be a fun few weeks.

CHAPTER FOUR

THE RAIN HAS NEARLY STOPPED as we pull into the diner's parking lot. Taking deep, calming breaths, I attempt to convince myself that my mood didn't cause the short but drenching downpour. My father's gift to me, the power to control water, could possibly wreak havoc if I don't learn to better control it.

As Cooper puts the SUV in park, we all climb out. Thanks to Abby's dad's extravagant tastes, we all rode comfortably, Wyck having been forced into the third row. Better his ill humor than the constant bickering between him and Easton. Sharing a seat, even with me between them (no, especially with me between them) might have proven fatal for one or both of them.

Only a few cars litter the parking lot. It's past rush hour so we should just about have the place to ourselves. Since there is nowhere else to eat within fifty miles, the diner is our only option for a hot meal. Besides, I'm hoping Julie will be working so that I can say goodbye the right way and to test my theory about Griffin's involvement in Mr. Lewis's 'death.' According to Griffin, he performed a mission at the time of Mr. Lewis's shooting, probably reversing Mr. Lewis's death.

When we walk inside, Julie doesn't bother to look up from her food delivery, she just says, "Take a seat anywhere. I'll be with you in a second."

We find a large table near the back, and I crane my head to catch a glimpse of who's manning the grill, but I can't see anything over the pick-up window.

Julie is halfway across the room before she at last glances at us. She stops dead in her tracks, her mouth hanging open. As I stand and smile, she squeals and launches herself at me, hugging me in a grip as tight as Easton's.

"Vivian! I thought I'd never see you again!" She pulls back to assess me. "Where have you been? I thought this one had forced you to run away with him." She points absently at Easton.

I cringe and shrug, giving Easton a 'sorry' smile. "Yeah, about that, we're back together." When I first came to work at the diner, I told everyone that I was running from a bad relationship, which wasn't entirely a lie. But I left out the part about it being bad for *him*, not me. "I'm really sorry I had to leave on short notice. Some family stuff came up" — also, not entirely a lie — "and we had to leave town, at least for a while. We're taking off again in the morning. We just stopped in for a good meal and to say goodbye."

"So soon? Well, I'm really glad he didn't murder you and dispose of your body like the creeps do on those cop shows." She squeezes me again, and I hear Easton snort in irritation.

Pulling back, I reply, "He's not really like that, Julie."

"That's what they all say, Viv," she says, patting my arm.

"Uh, food. Think we could maybe get some of it?" Abby, cranky when she's hungry, pipes up from the table, drawing both our attention.

"Sure, sorry," Julie apologizes. "You guys want to hear the specials or see a menu?"

Before Julie begins her recitation of the specials, I interrupt and take a chance on my hunch about Mr. Lewis. On our week long excursion to get back here, I filled everyone in on what I believe was a trap designed to ensure our cooperation since Easton and I thought Hoyt would kill Abby and Cooper, just as he had Mr. Lewis, if we didn't join him without a fight.

"Is Mr. Lewis here? I'd like to pick up my last check if I could," I ask while we all hold our breath waiting to see if my guess is correct.

"Yeah, he should be. Alejandro isn't scheduled for another hour or so. Try the back." She nods and distributes silverware to the table. "Oh, but he's not felt so great since his episode, so he may not be in the best mood."

"His episode?" I ask.

"Oh yeah, you don't know. Right before you guys took off no one had seen him, remember? Well, turns out he had a bad fall down the steps of his basement. Alejandro found him the next day once we figured out where he lived. Looked awful! Face bruised and cut up, huge gash on his head!" She shuttered. "It's a wonder he surveyed it as his age."

I knew exactly what Mr. Lewis's injuries looked like because I'd seen them in my mind, horrible visions courtesy of Hoyt, all fabricated to make me think Mr. Lewis had been sacrificed for me. Mr. Lewis had treated me like his granddaughter, giving me a job and a place to sleep. I still care for him despite the fact that he is a Magnet and drew me to him on Hoyt's order. In the memory I stole from Tyler the guard, Mr. Lewis's grandson, he had obviously refused his full cooperation, knowing it would mean his death at Hoyt's hands. So on some level, he must have grown to care for me, too, or he wouldn't have been willing to die rather than complete his mission. I wasn't sure what I would say to him, but I knew I couldn't leave without seeing him first.

"That's terrible!" I pretend ignorance. "We got called away before we could find him. I'll go back and see him." I smile, masking my unease at what reaction I'll receive from him.

"Do you want me to go with you?" Easton asks, starting to rise before I reply.

"No, I'm fine," I say as I walk away.

"Why would she need you to go with her?" Julie asks ill-temperedly. Despite my reassurance, she clearly has decided Easton is a controlling, crazy boyfriend, destined to end up on a true crime show.

I can hear her remonstrating him when I push open the swinging door into the kitchen. Mr. Lewis, his back to the door, thinks I'm Julie as he begins to call out instructions on some guy's burger set up.

"Pickles, onions, mayo, Julie." He flips the patty on the grill. "Come on, girl. I haven't got all night. I need to start on tomorrow's desserts."

I grab a plate and all the fixings then step to his side. Only after he's slid the patty home on the bun does he look up and notice it's not Julie standing next to him. He nearly drops the plate. I quickly take it from him and set it on the counter beside me.

"Mr. Lewis," I begin, but before I say anymore, he pulls me into a hug to rival Julie's, pressing my head tight against his wide, greasy-aproned chest and kissing the top of my head.

"Vivian," he says through tears, "I thought he'd killed you."

"Mr. Lewis," I squeak out, "you're suffocating me."

"Oh sorry, honey. I can't believe you're here!" He releases me but holds onto my upper arms as though he's afraid I'll disappear before his eyes. "You escaped?"

When I nod, a big-bellied rumble erupts from him. "I knew you would! I knew it when I saw what you did to the storage room door! Hot damn! You bested that old bastard!" He pulls me to him again but releases me so quickly that I would have fallen if he hadn't retained his grip on my arms. "I didn't want to, honey. I never wanted to, but especially not after I met you. He forced me, said he'd hurt Julie and her family if I didn't draw you here. Then the others just sort of happened. It's strange. Your boyfriend, he was gonna find you eventually. It's like I could feel him gettin' closer and closer. I just sped it along a little, and I wasn't real sure how he'd react to seein' you again after thinkin' you were dead."

"You knew? You knew that he thought I was dead?"

He chuckles, humorlessly this time. "They know everything, honey, told me they set it up that way. Told me to make sure you were safe till they could catch you all in one big trap. Even tried to use Tyler to persuade me." He slaps his hands together as though he's shutting the trap himself then shakes his head regretfully. "I'm so sorry, Vivian."

"No, Mr. Lewis, it's okay. I mean, not *okay*, but I totally understand. I'm sorry they put you and Tyler in the middle." I reach up and touch the greenish-yellow bruising still visible on his face and forehead. "He showed me what he did to you. He made me think he'd killed you."

"I wondered as much, sick bastard! I always did hate him even when he was a nothin' piss ant teenager who couldn't even blow up a balloon, much less hurt anybody." He puts the burger on the window and dings the bell for Julie to pick it up. "So, he got himself a Twister, huh? Reversed time, did he?" He shakes his head again and stares off like he can see the future through the back wall of the kitchen. "He'll never stop."

"Tell me about him." I hop up on the counter beside the grill, pushing aside a towel resting there and wiggling until my feet don't touch the floor. Without responding, he moves toward a large mixing bowl on my other side. He begins to put in pre-sorted ingredients.

"I need to know. I can't fight him if you don't tell me." I touch his weathered hand, and he gazes up, meeting my eyes as though he's assessing my value, whether I can handle his truth or not.

Nodding his head once, he begins, "Do you know what he is to you, what relation?" At my hesitant nod, he continues. "Good, that's good 'cause if you've already learned that and haven't run stark-ravin' crazy, there's hope for you yet." He grins with one side of his mouth then winces and touches his bruised cheek. "How much do you know about your daddy?"

"Not much, just what my friend could steal from the confidential personnel files." I shrug. "I know he was a Water Element, Hoyt's brother, and a coward who seduced my mother then left the two us to fend for ourselves." I don't bother to hide my anger over his betrayal.

He clucks his tongue reprovingly, sounding like an old mother hen. "Ah"—he swats my knee—"here I thought you were smarter than that, Vivian! Your daddy wasn't like that at all! Yeah, he was a Water Element, a damn good one, and yeah, he was brother to that crazy SOB, but that part about your mother? Well, that ain't right at all."

He begins stirring the contents of the bowl with a long, wooden spoon just as Julie flies up to the window and slaps down an order.

"Order up, all except for Vivian's part. You can write that on yourself," she says, as she flounces away to gather cups and ice.

Handing me the bowl and spoon, he motions for me to keep stirring while he reads over the order. He whips into motion like a well-oiled machine, starting the orders. Raising his eyebrows at me, he looks down at the order.

Realizing he wants to know what I want, I shake my head. "Anything's fine. I'm more interested in what you mean about my mom and dad than I am in eating." He continues his preparation. "Mr. Lewis, I'm dying here. Tell me please!"

But he just waves me off. "In a second, girl, not like someone's chasin' ya." He laughs at his own joke, and I can't help but smile. I genuinely like this man, and once again, I puzzle over how his grandson, Tyler, could be so brainwashed against him.

After what feels like forever and my arm has turned to jelly from stirring, he turns to me as he takes out cake pans and places them beside me on the counter. He motions for me to pour in the batter after he's greased and floured them. Dipping his finger in the left-over batter clinging to the inside of the mixing bowl, he closes his eyes and tastes.

"That's good stuff. Try it," he commands as he opens his eyes. "My own recipe, lemon with strawberry glaze. Here," he says, hand-ing me another bowl and more ingredients from the fridge. "Mix these while I finish your friends' meal." He places the cake pans in the oven and turns back to the grill.

I sigh but do as instructed, adding and stirring automatically as he begins again.

"See, sweetheart, baking is all about finding the right combina-tion of ingredients. Too little of this, and it's too bitter. Too much of that, and it's too sweet. You have to work to get it just right." His face serious, he looks at me again. "That's the way it was with your mother and father. Your father, he was," he pauses and glances up before smiling, "well, he was of the too sweet variety. Where your uncle was bold and grasping, your father was kind and loving. When he was assigned to your mother" — he stops my stirring with a touch on my hand — "he didn't want to do it. He refused for a while until your uncle took matters into his own hands. I'm not sure how he eventually forced your dad into goin' after her, but he did. So, he courted your mom. I can't say for sure how he felt about her, but he sure looked like he loved her, followed her around like a whipped puppy." He smiles at a distant memory, and turns back to the grill.

"I wasn't there when you were born. I'd been sent away on a mis-sion." He shakes his head and flips a steak. "When I returned, they were gone — your dad, your mom, and, apparently, you."

As he plates the food and dings the bell for Julie to pick it up, I absently stir what I assume is the glaze for his cake, wondering if Mr. Lewis has it right. Could my dad have loved my mom after all? If he did, why would he ever agree to leave her? And leave her he did. Hoyt's memories showed me that.

He takes the bowl from my hands and helps me hop off the counter. "Will they come after you again?" I ask as I take in his warm eyes and gray hair. He kisses my forehead.

"Doesn't matter. Someone beat him, and now I can die a happy man." Releasing me, he gives my back a tiny shove toward the kitchen door. "Go eat before your food gets cold."

"What did you fix me?" I ask before pushing open the door.

"You'll have to see for yourself." He removes the cake pans and begins prodding them with a toothpick to see if they are done.

"So, it's a surprise, huh?" I smile at him.

Lifting his head, he chuckles. "The best things always are."

CHAPTER FIVE

First Mission

Terror in his eyes,
my eyes,
as he scrambles up the embankment.
I grasp his outstretched hand,
but mine,
slick with blood not my own,
finds no grip.
Before he slips down beyond my reach again,
I slide forward, knees digging,
gravel and debris cutting through my shirt.
We grunt in unison,
a soldier's ballad,
until we lie, breaths harsh, arms touching,
along the edge.
Though the scrapes on his face are already healing,
I fear his expression may never
as he stares at my hands
then his own,
covered in another man's crimson.
"I can't believe you did that."
His tone's loud even over the crackling pops

of the burning house
so close the gust of flames
singe my lungs, make my eyes water.
"He would have done the same to us."
But he shakes his head,
the green of eyes
stark against his scrapes.
"What have you done?"
"I've saved us, brother."

CHAPTER SIX

BY THE TIME I RETURN TO THE TABLE, the others are devouring their food. Easton looks up from his steak and smiles.

"Thought I'd have to eat yours, too," he says, nodding toward an enormous cheeseburger with onion rings piled into a crispy, golden mountain on the side. Mr. Lewis remembered that was my favorite.

When I fail to return Easton's smile, his brows draw together with concern. "You okay, babe?" He pulls out my chair, and I slide into it, grabbing my napkin-wrapped utensils.

"I'm fine." I try to smile, but the effort falls short somehow. "Eat. We'll talk later." I stop the conversation before he can question me further. I need time to digest everything Mr. Lewis told me. He seems to think my father loved my mother, but was it all part of the trap? Did he put up a front so that my mother would be fooled, too? She wouldn't be the first woman to fall for that.

"OMG! This is so good!" Abby groans with pleasure. "I thought I'd never eat anything but beef jerky and peanuts again!" She laughs as she scoops up a big forkful of mashed potatoes with brown gravy then turns to Cooper, fork raised. "You've got to try this," she commands, popping the fork into his open mouth.

"Umm..." Coop closes his eyes to savor the taste, and I'm flooded with guilt again that something as simple as this could give them both such joy. If it weren't for me, they would never have been living from a backpack for the past week.

"Oh, you have a little on your face." Abby leans over to kiss a spot near his mouth. I'm not positive, but I'm pretty sure she just licked him. Before I can roll my eyes, Wyck pretends to gag from his seat next to me.

"Ugh! Get a room you two! Must we endure that while we eat?" he asks, shaking his head.

Abby giggles and kisses Coop lightly on the mouth while he smiles. "You're just jealous," Coop says, feeding Abby a piece of his steak.

Wyck lifts one eyebrow. "Jealous? Please. All I have to do is wait for Vivian to fall asleep, and she supplies me with all the... affection I need." He clears his throat smugly and takes a drink of his iced tea.

On my other side, Easton stiffens and moves to push away from the table, presumably to go after Wyck, but I put my hand on his arm and give him a pleading look before turning to Wyck. I touch his arm, too, but in a very different way.

"I thought we had a deal." I send a tiny zap into his bare forearm.

He yanks it away. "Damn! Stop doing that!" Rubbing his tingling skin, he grumps, "Yeah, yeah, truce or get fried. I remember." But he leans in so close his lips brush my ear as he whispers, "Let's just hope *you* remember that when you snuggle up in bed tonight."

Me, too. I don't understand this thing with Wyck, but I need to get away from him soon for both Easton's and my sake. Once I help him find his mother, he's on his own.

The remainder of the meal passes with only the clinking of silverware and a few satisfied burps. When Julie comes to clear the plates, I glance around and notice we're the only customers left in the diner.

"Who wants dessert?" she chirps perkily as she brings out the cake Mr. Lewis and I baked together while he talked about my family. We all groan at the thought, but everyone takes one of the small plates as she cuts the yellow and pink masterpiece. The heavenly flavor explodes on my tongue when I take my first bite, and my eyes close seemingly of their own accord at the taste. Mr. Lewis's heavy hand on my shoulder forces them back open.

"How is it, kids? It's a new recipe, and you guys are my guinea pigs," he says, smiling proudly because he can tell from our expressions it is beyond great.

"It's amazing!" Abby exclaims. "It may be the best cake I've ever eaten." A big boast for the girl who once claimed she could live on cupcakes.

The others all nod and yum their approvals until our stomachs are full to bursting. Before Julie begins to clear the plates from the table again, she leans down and hugs me, her cheek pressing against mine. "In case I don't see you again anytime soon." She hurriedly swipes at her cheek when she rises and picks up my plate.

"Bye, Julie," I reply as she rushes away with the dishes. I can't really say Julie and I were super-close. We only saw each other at work, but I can say she was my friend, and I'll miss her.

Cooper rises from the table and offers Abby his hand. "We should get back to the motel if we're headin' out early tomorrow." He takes his wallet from his back pocket.

"Put that away, boy. This one's on me." Mr. Lewis waves away Coop's money. When Cooper opens his mouth to protest, Mr. Lewis says, "Call it a going-away present for one of my best employees. Besides, I owe her one." He smiles warmly down at me, and I push away from the table.

"You guys go ahead. I want to say goodbye then I'll walk back to the motel." But Easton's having none of that.

"No way you're walking back alone. You three go. I'll stay with Vivian." He nods to Cooper who leans across to shake Mr. Lewis's hand.

"Thank you, sir," he says, and Abby waves as she turns to go. Wyck, his expression tight as though he wants to argue, finally steps toward the door when I raise one eyebrow in warning.

"I can't thank you enough, Mr. Lewis." I take his hand in mine. "I'm really, really sorry that you had to get mixed up in all of this."

He grips my hand. "What'd I tell you in the kitchen? I don't give two cents about that. It was all worth it to see Commander Matthews," he sneers the name, "get what was comin' to him."

"Well, I'm not sure he has—yet—but he will if I ever see him again. That I promise." I realize I mean exactly that, surprised by the sudden rush of fury in my gut. If I see him again, I won't hesitate. We still have a reckoning.

"Oh, I'd say you knocked him down a peg or two." He chuckles. "Wish I could've seen it." He shakes his head and pulls his hand from mine. "No matter." His face turns serious as he hesitates, seeming as though he doesn't want to say what he's about to say. "Vivian, if you see my grandson again, don't tell him I'm alive. It'll only make him believe even harder in the greatness of Commander

Matthews." His heavy brows draw together sharply. "He'll think the man was being generous when all he was really doin' was savin' me for another mission."

"But—" I begin. He holds up his hand with finality.

"No, now you listen to me. Don't tell him. You're a good person, and you'll be tempted to, but don't." He swallows hard. "You and I both have done things we wish we could take back," he mutters, his eyes probing into mine as though he can see the blond swimmer I helped to drown after my first mission. My uncle forced me to use my water Gift to pull the man away from shore, and he died for some stupid political power play. I drop my gaze, unable to meet his stare any longer. "But you can't dwell on those things," he says in a low voice. I remember Hoyt saying something similar, and I wonder, when Hoyt first began, if he ever did. Did he have a conscience at some point that pained him when he took a life? Or was he evil from the beginning? The opposite of my caring father, if what Mr. Lewis said is true.

I can feel Easton's curious gaze on my face. He still doesn't know what I did. I have to tell him soon.

Mr. Lewis bends and kisses me on the forehead before pulling me in for another bear hug. He turns to Easton. "You keep her safe, boy. Take care of her, and be the distraction she'll need very soon."

Easton nods at Mr. Lewis's cryptic words and shakes the hand he offers. All three of us know that it's more likely I will have to take care of Easton, physically at least. But mentally, I've come to rely on Easton for his strength, and Mr. Lewis must sense that, too.

"You two have a connection that goes beyond the present. It's very strong." He tilts his head, examining us like some strange, new recipe. "It goes back a long way." A smile spreads across his face, and he nods knowingly. "There is much more to your bond than you realize." He tweaks my nose then puts a hand on each of our shoulders. "Have fun discovering it." He picks up the cake still sitting on the table, grabs a small piece, and takes a bite. Shaking his head in pleasure, he walks away mumbling, "The sweetest rewards come from the biggest risks, Vivian."

CHAPTER SEVEN

STEPPING OUT FROM THE COOL DINER, the air closes in like a muggy blanket. The motel is only a half-mile walk, but the thick, close night makes it seem much farther. Easton's reassuring hand in mine swings lightly between us as though he's not dying to know what Mr. Lewis was talking about when he said we had both 'done things' that we can never take back. While he has yet to say anything, I can feel the vibe pulsating from his mind. I promised him I wouldn't invade his thoughts, but I don't have to with the volume of his questions.

"Just ask already," I say irritably, stopping on the sidewalk. "And don't even try to act like you don't want to know."

Taken aback by my stinging tone, he doesn't immediately reply. "Fine. What have you done that you wish you could take back?"

"I... was forced to..." I thought I was ready to get this over with, tell him everything, but now that the moment has arrived, I'm not sure I can.

"To what?" he prompts, crossing his arms and tilting his head skeptically, not about to let me weasel out now.

I run my hands through my hair for a moment's reprieve. Then I take a death breath; he deserves to know so he can leave now if he wants instead of going along with the girl who killed a man she didn't even know.

"I killed a man, Easton." His eyes widen, but his stance doesn't change, so I hurry on. "Hoyt forced me to help him drown this guy—a guy who was minding his own business, going for his morning swim—all because of his politics." It all comes pouring out like a faucet left running. "After we went to collect that kid, I told you about him, Zeb the Fire Element, Hoyt took me with him to some beach. He told me he would kill Abby if I didn't do it. He made me help him drown this man. We used our powers and killed him because the Liaisons had been hired to get rid of him. He probably had a family, kids even, and friends who don't understand how he drowned."

Closing my eyes, I can still see his shiny blond hair and tan skin, the picture of health, nodding to me as he readied for his swim. Then I see that golden head going down for the final time, the ocean covering him. "I never told you because I didn't know how to say it or how you'd feel about having a girlfriend who murdered someone."

Feeling sick, I turn from him and cover my mouth with my hand; the burger and rings threaten to make a reappearance. My knees give, and I sink to the sidewalk. "I'm as bad as my uncle." I grunt soberly. "The apple doesn't fall far, huh?"

He paces behind me, and I'm tempted to slip inside his head to hear his thoughts. When I can't take it anymore, I glare at him. "Say something, Easton!"

He crouches beside me, his face turned away from me so that I can't read his expression. "You should have told me, Vivian. You should have told me before I had to ask."

"I know," I murmur, dropping my eyes to the fingers I'm twisting in my lap.

"Does he know?" he asks too quietly.

"Who? Mr. Lewis?" His question catches me off guard, and I chance a glance at him. His expression is as hard as granite, his jaw set and menacing.

"Wyck? Did you tell him already?" His eyes narrow, and his lips tighten into a line.

It takes me a second to process what he's asking. I've just agonized my way through the darkest secret I hope to ever have, and all he's concerned about is his stupid, asinine jealousy of Wyck?

"Is that all you're worried about? I spill a secret that's been eating at me like a cancer, and that's all you have to say?" I feel my temper escalate, and my power amp slightly, despite the fact that I've nearly exhausted it in the stress of the last couple of weeks. My voice shakes. "No, Easton, I didn't tell Wyck. I haven't told anyone but you, not even Mr. Lewis. This jealous side of you lost its cuteness days ago. This is about me, not you! Get over yourself!" I jump up. "I need to be alone. *Don't* follow me."

I run without thought until my lungs burn, my rubbery legs taking me down some forgotten road on the outskirts of town. When I collapse to the dusty ground, I can't stop the tears. I've always hated to cry. Crying never solves anything; it just leaves me exhausted with red eyes and a stuffy nose, but I don't have any fight left for this. So, the tears trek unchecked down my cheeks and splash in tiny circles on my jeans. Knees drawn up, I rest my head against them and sob.

I'm so tired of all this—the running, the hiding, the searching, and now Easton's insecurity! I wish I could reverse the last six months, go back to my home and let Aunt Charlotte make me coffee, hear her tell me it's all going to work out.

"Well, well, well, what do we have here?"

I jerk upright and search the darkness around me. The disembodied, female voice laughs cruelly.

"I'm over here," the voice taunts from somewhere in front of me.

Squinting into the moonless night, I can make out only the outline of a few trees along the road. Standing, I turn in a circle, probing the blackness for the voice's owner.

"Not there. I'm over here." Again the voice laughs, but this time it's behind me, and a spark of recognition ignites in my head. I know that voice.

Whipping around, I call on every ounce of strength I have left until my palm begins to glow a soft blue. I won't be full force, but I also won't be helpless. Right about now, I'm wishing I had my enhancer, the device I conned Carter into making and which Wyck later stole for me. I used it to drain Hoyt's brain and to help us escape, and I've kept it in a pocket of my backpack ever since, hesitant to use it again, but I would definitely feel better if I had it strapped across my hand while I face this unseen voice.

"Oh no, Vivian's getting upset!" says the voice in mock fear.

"Lilah? Is that you?" I spin around again, searching for her. Her body begins to materialize before me, shimmering and wavy for a moment before becoming clear.

"Miss me, bitch?" she sneers, hands on her vinyl-clad hips. With her blue and black hair pulled into a tight, high ponytail, she looks as villainous as always. "What? No hug?" she asks as she sashays toward me in her knee-high biker boots and tight yellow t-shirt.

"How's the head, Lilah?" I ask, reminding her of our last encounter when I used her skull to open a window.

She smirks and holds her hand out in front of her as though she's checking her manicure. "How's your aunt? Still dead?"

I reach out to grab her, fearing my power isn't strong enough to hurt her without touching her, but when my hand swipes right through her, I stumble forward and am forced to take a steadying step before I whip back around to face her again.

Lilah cackles maniacally as her form ripples slightly. "Dumb ass! The look on your face!" She laughs again before her expression sobers. She begins to circle me slowly like she's got all night. "If I were really here, you'd be dead already." Her lip curls in a feral grin. "I'd have slit your pathetic throat while you bawled in the road."

"How did you find me? And how are you doing this?" Breath saws rapidly in and out of my chest as my eyes scan the road and the trees beyond. Lilah must be close if she is able to use her Magician abilities to create this illusion. If she's close, then Hoyt and his men must be. He would never allow her to go alone on a mission. Even Hoyt knows that Lilah's a loose cannon. I suspect he's only keeping her around until he can replace her. Her attitude is a liability to a control freak like my uncle. He'll never fully dominate her, and that makes her dangerous.

She smiles, her red lips a slash across her face, as she steps in close again. Her green, kohl-lined eyes glitter, catching what little starlight there is. "Scared?"

When I don't respond, she moves her hands rapidly. I flinch back, forgetting she isn't flesh and blood. She snickers again then looks over her shoulder at someone I can't see. "Yeah, yeah, I'll tell her!" She turns back to me and mutters, "Can't even have a little fun. You ruined everything! Why couldn't you just do what you were commanded?" She takes a deep breath. Almost petulantly like a child who's been sent to her room, she says, "I'm a projection, sent by the commander."

"Sent? If he can project to me, he must know where I am. Why didn't he come himself?" I ask warily.

"He can't," she replies, but as she utters the words, she screams and grabs her head in pain. "Sorry, sorry, please stop!" she pleads. Then it becomes clear to me what's happening. While he is strong enough to send a message via Lilah, he hasn't physically recovered enough to leave the facility, and he doesn't want me to see him. He must somehow be tapping into her Magician powers and using them to enhance his strength, forcing her to create the illusion of herself that he then projects to me. She's his puppet until he regains his full power, and I'm unable to block him until I regain mine.

"You will see him soon." She pants, still holding her head. "He warns you not to search for your father. He says you won't be happy with what you find. After all, your father seduced your whore mother." Again, she clutches her head and doubles over. "Okay, I'm sorry!" She isn't talking to me, and I wonder briefly why Hoyt would punish her for saying that. Maybe he just doesn't want her to deviate from the script he's feeding her. When she's able to stand, she continues, her voice tight and less forceful. "You're only endangering your friends and yourself. If you stop and return to the facility, he will forgive you, and you'll resume training. Your friends will be free."

Right. "Does he really expect me to believe that?"

"Just do what he wants, Vivian," she replies, her eyes boring into mine, and for the first time since I had the displeasure of meeting Lilah, I sense her fear, pure and raw. Not even when I squeezed her in an energy rope or when Griffin stabbed her on the plane did I see terror like I see now. She fears Hoyt and what he'll do to all of us. While I completely empathize, I won't give up.

"I can't," I whisper, shaking my head.

"He won't stop. You'll kill us all," she whimpers as her body ripples and shimmers, fading from view.

CHAPTER EIGHT

Reason

"You must do it."
But he shakes his head,
shaggy, dark blond hair
falling over his brows and nearly
into his eyes, once my eyes.
"It's wrong, and I won't."
When he stands eye level with me,
I know I have only one choice.
He hates what I'm becoming;
he doesn't need to say it.
I hear it
without his words.
He hates what I'm learning,
he doesn't understand
that I've pushed myself
for us,
to protect us,
to make us necessary.
He hates what we've been told,
he doesn't comprehend
that leaving

is not an option.
He hates not being normal.
The life he wants—
the white fence, the brick house, the two kids—
can only be
a fairytale for us.
We are too much for the world
outside these rock walls.
His jealousy
that the soldiers may come and go
permeates our lives.
What could he do on the outside?
He knows only a feeble service
to the cause,
no survival instinct.
He isn't even a fit soldier.
He is kindness,
and compassion,
and weakness.
Who will watch over him
(he, who cannot hurt a fly)
on the outside?
I have done the things
I knew he could not.
But the others,
they grow weary,
tired of his excuses,
tired of his heart.
He is not the machine
they wanted,
not the machine
they engineered.
I must force him to see,
to realize,
the consequences of
uselessness.
The cause has no conscience.

For his own good.
Even if he hates me more,
he will be alive.
"You will, or they will do far worse."
"She is a human being,
not a mission!"
"Not to us, brother."
"If I do this, I will be killing a part of myself."
"If you do not, you will be killing her."
At his retreating back,
I say the one thing that will forever
damn me in his heart
but save both their lives.
"I've seen her,
spoken to her,
pretended to be you."
Hand on the doorknob,
he stills and slowly faces me,
his green eyes flash
with fury
as he gracefully catches
my dark sunglasses.
"With those.
"Pretending to love her will not be a
great hardship."
"What have you done?"
"I've saved you, brother,
if you will carry through
with the mission.
If not,
I will return to her
one last time."
Head hanging
in defeat,
his voice quiet,
he will not meet my eyes.
"I'd hoped

that it was only your eyes,
but your heart
has become black
as well."
"Perhaps,
but I will always choose
your life over hers."
"Soon, you'll not be able
to hide your evil
behind sunglasses, *brother*."

CHAPTER NINE

I PULL THE KEY from my pocket and slide it into the lock. Turning the knob as quietly as possible, I open the door and quickly slip inside the dark room, trying not to wake Abby. On my walk back to the motel, I replayed Lilah's visit over and over in my head. Hoyt must be badly injured if he hasn't come for me yet, but he wants me to know that he knows where we are, or he would never have sent Lilah's image to me.

The sight of her bent in pain from his brutal mental punishment reinforces my fear for Abby, Cooper, and Easton. He wants me back to carry out his sick missions, but it's more than that. He doesn't want me to find my father, his brother. Was he being honest when he said I wouldn't like what I found, or was it just another fear tactic? I have to recharge and work on blocking him again; otherwise, we won't get far. I can't let him get into my head.

Briefly I wonder about Easton. He wasn't where I left him, so I assume he must be in his room with Cooper. I don't know what I'll say to him when I see him tomorrow. 'Hey, sorry I dropped a truth bomb on you then left you last night.' Somehow, I don't think that is going to cut it. Will he forgive me for what I've done? And I don't mean leaving him on the sidewalk.

Exhaustion makes my feet feel like lead blocks as I raise them one at a time to take off my Converses and socks. I need sleep. I have to rest to get my strength back. I slip out of my jeans but leave on my t-shirt. Abby and I will be sharing the only bed in the room, but we've slumber-partied at each other's houses, lying side-by-side to keep from waking her parents or Aunt Charlotte, and giggled ourselves to sleep so many times it doesn't matter.

Briefly, I consider searching my bag for my pajama pants, but I don't want to wake Abby by turning on the light. I can barely make out a still form on the bed, and I can hear soft breathing. We *all* need to sleep. I wonder if Easton is sleeping as soundly. I suppress a snicker at the thought of Easton, Cooper, and Wyck sharing a room. Something tells me they aren't all sharing a bed like Abby and I are. Like wrestling a straightjacket, I pull my arms inside my shirt and slip off my bra, laying it on top of my jeans, then I lift the covers and slide into bed. The sheets are rough but cool and clean, and I sigh into my pillow.

"What took you so long?" Easton's deep, melodic voice startles me just as I'm closing my eyes.

I sit up quickly, trying without success to see his face in the dark, and squeak, "Easton? What are you doing in here? Where's Abby?"

I can hear his smile. "Nice to see you, too, babe." His delicious, low chuckle sends a shudder up my back and not in a bad way.

"I can't see you... uh... didn't see you I mean... I didn't expect... I thought... shit!" Easton laughs. I'm floundering, and he's amused. I take a deep breath, which does nothing to calm my racing pulse, but at least I'm able to speak coherently. "Abby and I are supposed to be sharing this room. I wasn't expecting you." My eyes finally adjust enough that I can make out the outline of his head and shoulders as he sits up, too.

His laughter dies to a snort. "So I noticed. If you want me to leave, I will," he says, his voice drops, becoming all melted chocolate-smoothness, "but I don't really want to."

Okay. "I guess Abby, Cooper, and Wyck are sharing a room. That's gotta be... awkward." I ignore his last statement because I don't really know if I want him to go or not. Part of me doesn't want him to leave, but another part, the part that can see Aunt Charlotte's pursed lips and narrowed eyes, does. My mind flashes to her flustered face when she caught Easton and me in my room last spring after I explained my abilities to him. No, she would be less than pleased with my current location.

"Abby and Cooper are. This was her little plan. She claimed she wasn't feeling well and wanted Cooper there in case she got sick.

They were already camped out in the other room when I got back. She has a devious little mind, doesn't she?" He laughs again then stops short. "I have no idea where the dickhead is. I think I saw him headed to Abby's car."

"Oh." I let it drop. I don't want to fight about Wyck right now. I sigh, and he reaches out in the dark and rubs my arm. "Easton, I'm sorry. I'm sorry for leaving you tonight, I'm sorry I didn't tell you sooner about the guy, I'm sorry you're sleeping in a motel instead of at home in your own bed, I'm just... sorry."

He tucks me into his side, my head resting on his shoulder. My foggy brain briefly registers that he isn't wearing a shirt. "I'm not angry with you for taking off. I was out of line. You were right. I should've been focused on what you were telling me, not on whether anyone else knew. I've been a jerk lately, and I'm sorry, too. I'm just so jealous of the time you've spent with him." I start to argue, but he stops me. "I know I can trust you, but I don't trust him, babe, and I think he'd do just about anything to have you. And he has power, a way to help you when I can't. I'm grateful for his saving you, but I'm furious that it wasn't me." I can hear the pain in his voice.

So this is the nitty-gritty. Easton hates that Wyck is able to do something he can't. I remember how helpless he felt when he was locked away in the prison quarters and the awful fight we had about it. He wants to brawl with Wyck all the time because it's the 'manly' way to fight what he can't really fight—his feelings of insecurity. I'll bet this is the first time in his life he's been unsure of himself.

"And I don't want you to beat yourself up over what you did." He gently scolds me as he caresses my arm where it's wrapped around his waist. "I know you were protecting all of us, not just Abby. You did what you had to. I would never leave you for that." He stops rubbing my arms and shifts so that my head is lying on the pillow, and he is propped on his elbow, gazing down at me. I can't see his eyes, but I know there's no anger in them. "I love you, remember?" I graze my fingers across the stubble on his jaw and then across his lips, feeling his breath, before he takes my hand in his and brushes his lips against my palm.

My body goes all kinds of tingly, and my palm and eyes begin to glow softly. The beauty of his face, illuminated by the soft gray light, takes my breath as he lowers his lips to mine. The rational part of my brain begins to clear her throat, reminding me not to let this get out of hand, but my hormones sit up and begin to pant.

When he deepens the kiss, he skims his hand down my arm to my hip, and I raise my hands to his neck, sliding them into his thick hair. His lips glide to my ear where I hear his ragged breathing, then down my neck as his hand slips to my bare leg. He groans and squeezes my leg tenderly, and suddenly, I'm very aware that I am nearly naked and in a bed with a completely eatable boy.

Rational brain begins to shake hormone brain, and she's about to win when Easton brings his lips back to mine and slides his hand along the hem of my shirt. As his fingers sweep against my stomach underneath, hormone brain begins to do the happy dance on top of rational brain.

His lips move down my neck again, leaving goose bumps in his wake while his hand moves to my ribs, barely touching, but enough to cause a current to race between us. Something about this male makes me feel alive, energized, and my hand glows brighter. Well, this is one way to recharge. He groans again, and the sound does strange things to my insides.

"Vivian, do you feel that?" he pants as his lips dip to the v-neck of my shirt. He looks into my eyes. "It's your energy. I feel it." His blue-green eyes darken.

"It's *our* energy," I whisper. He sits up quickly, pulling me along with him, and both of his hands slide beneath my shirt, skimming my ribs and the tender underside of my arms as he pulls it over my head. His warm chest pressed against mine, he kisses me as though both our lives depended on it. It's fierce and possessive. His love, fear, and jealousy, explode in that one moment, and I am helpless against the power it imparts. I kiss him back, trying to show him how much I need his strength, how much I need him.

He shifts us both so that I'm again lying on my back. His elbows support his upper body and his hands cup my face while he presses himself against me. At the feel of his shorts against my inner thighs, rational brain pummels hormone brain like a heavy-weight boxer.

Do I want this to happen? Yes! No... I don't know. This is not something I take lightly. I love Easton more than I think he realizes, but this is a life-altering event, something that will stay with me forever. Do I want to remember it this way? In a sleazy motel room, the threat of Hoyt Matthews looming ever-present and insidious in the background? When Easton skims his hand down my shoulder to my chest, hormone brain throws her battered self against the inside of my head, screaming, 'Yes, you do!'

His mouth follows his hand, and I'm a bundle of sensitivity, my skin singing and burning with his touch. I hear him gasp my name, and I slide my azure hand up his back, the muscles bunching beneath my touch, and he winces slightly then moans. His mouth slips wetly back to my lips where he kisses me deeply then pulls back to peer into my eyes.

"Vivian, I want this so much. I want *you* so much, but—I can't believe I'm about to say this." He shakes his head and sighs, his breath hot and minty on my face. "Something doesn't feel right. You don't really want this to happen right now. I don't know how I know; I just feel it, and if you aren't ready, I'm not ready. I want this moment to be perfect." He rolls to his back and throws his arm across his eyes as though he's disgusted with his chivalry.

I'm momentarily stunned. Hormone brain is now in the fetal position, crying obscenely, while rational brain is high-fiving herself. What the heck?! Have I just been rejected? But then Easton's words sink in. He can sense that I'm unsure, and even though he wants me, he has done what I didn't. The thought warms me and makes me smile. He loves me enough to stop what he knows isn't right for us at the moment.

"Ugh! I'm an embarrassment to every guy on the planet! I'm in bed with a gorgeous girl with a killer body, who makes me weak when she whispers my name, and I tell her we can't!" He's mumbling, almost to himself. His breath is still sawing heavily from between his lips.

Pulling the sheet up to my chin, I lean over him, grinning like a fool. I lift his arm from his eyes. But his are squeezed shut in humiliation.

"Hey, open your eyes," I coax, running my fingers along the planes of his cheeks, his nose, his forehead. When he finally looks at me, I smile sweetly and say, "Thank you."

Raising his eyebrows, he looks quizzically at me. "You're thanking me? Why?"

"For being so sweet." He huffs out a breath. "You knew I wasn't sure, and you stopped us. Thank you." I lean down to kiss his cheek.

He puts his arms around me and presses my ear to his chest. I can hear his heartbeat as it returns to normal. His lips brush against the top of my head.

"It's an important decision, one I've taken too lightly in the past, and I don't want that for you... with you. I want you to be sure and not just caught up in the heat of the moment." He groans lightly. "And it was definitely a heated moment, babe." I can hear rather than see his sexy-as-hell grin as he runs his hands up and down my back, sending little shivers dancing along my skin. I move my leg on top of one of his and rub against his calf with my foot. I kiss his chest and gaze up at him, my eyes and palm slowly returning to normal. "Do you really think I'm gorgeous?" I ask, my fingers tracing tiny circles on his hard pecs.

He shifts his lower body uncomfortably. "Of course. I probably don't tell you that enough. Why do you think it makes me so crazy when that douche bag looks at you?"

Ignoring his comment about Wyck, I continue my torturous inquisition. Just because we can't do the deed doesn't mean we can't fool around. Hormone brain rubs her hands together in delightful anticipation. "And you think I have a nice body?" I move so that more of my skin is touching more of his, and he rewards me with a groan.

"No, not a nice body—a killer body." Easton's breathing is picking back up, and his hand begins to tug slowly on the sheet covering me.

I nip his ear with my teeth and whisper, "Easton." When he flips me over and begins kissing me fervently, rational brain shakes her head, knowing I will not be sleeping much tonight.

CHAPTER TEN

A BILLOWY, WHITE LACE CURTAIN. A breeze scented with pine, fresh air, and home. A patchwork quilt swirling with tiny flowers, soft from years of happy dreams. A feeling of contentment and safety. A man's voice as comforting as my bed. "Time to wake up, sleepyhead."

* * *

I blink against the harsh, afternoon light blazing through the window. When I try to sit up, my back cramps, and my legs ache with pins and needles. We've been in this SUV for so long I think my butt has grown roots to the leather seat. Since we left two days ago, we've driven in shifts. We haven't stopped driving except for bathroom breaks, gas, and food. Easton turns to me from the behind the wheel and smiles.

"Hey, have a good nap?" he asks, reaching for my hand.

I nod and stretch before peeking between the seats to find Abby curled and snoozing cozily in Cooper's arms. Solving the mystery of Stonehenge would be easier than figuring out how Coop is managing to sleep, long legs squeezed up in the seat and arms wrapped around Abby. One of them is snoring softly, and I grin, remembering the fight they had a few hours ago over the merits of country music versus pop. Coop, bellowing some twangy, she's-leaving-me song, only turned the radio up louder when Abby complained. She then pulled the 'it's my car' rationale and switched it to the whining of the latest boy wonder with a lame haircut. After a small skirmish in which the auxiliary cord was pitched to the back of the SUV (striking Wyck in the head by the way), Easton ordered a pit stop and a driver change.

"Guess they made up, huh?" I whisper so as not to wake the sleepers and start round two.

Grinning, he says, "I suppose. They were asleep about five minutes after you."

I crane my neck slightly and catch a glimpse of Wyck, who is stretched across the farthest seat, one arm under his head, the other hanging over the edge of the seat, and both feet propped against the window.

"How much farther do you think it is?" I turn back to face the highway and the built-in GPS unit in Abby's console.

"We're close, I think. I hope Wyck knows what he's talking about." Easton shakes his head.

"Me, too." I glance in the rearview mirror where I can see Wyck, still sleeping peacefully. The closer we get to the end of our journey, the quieter and more withdrawn he's become, barely speaking to any of us. "It must be really hard, Easton, not knowing for sure where your mom is or if she's even still alive. At least I know for sure, you know?"

"Yeah, I can't stand the guy, but I hope we find her—alive and well." He pulls my hand to his mouth and softly brushes his lips across my knuckles.

"All we have is the address he stole from the confidential files in the facility, his mom's last known address. He didn't even know they'd moved her from the house where he and Griffin grew up." I state feeling slightly queasy at the thought that we may come up empty handed. "He needs closure, one way or another."

"But what happens when we do find her?" he asks, glancing from the road to me.

Gazing out the window at an ancient barn where several horses graze lazily, I hedge. "I don't know. Guess we'll find out soon, huh?" I've wondered the same thing about a thousand times since we left the motel. I don't know how Wyck will ever protect her or where they will go because he won't be able to just leave her there. The Liaisons and Hoyt will never allow that. He swore that he would help me find my dad, but if we find her alive, I don't want him to leave her behind, and I don't want to put Wyck at risk if he's all she really has left. Griffin's crossed over to the dark side as far as I'm concerned.

Easton nods then bites his bottom lip and peeks shyly over at me. I know where this is headed. We still haven't really talked about what happened our last night at the motel. "So, this is our first chance to talk about... you know... what happened."

I pull a page from his book, remembering how coy he'd been after our prom fiasco when I had tried to explain Aunt Charlotte's well-meaning gift, the box of condoms she'd stuck in my purse. "Oh really, what exactly happened? Refresh my memory." Trying to hide my smile, I look out at an old gas station squatting on a forgotten square of green.

Pursing his lips, he shrugs. "Well, there was some kissing, some touching, some—"

Putting my hand over his mouth, I stop him before he completely embarrasses me even though no one else is listening. Giggling, I whisper, "Someone will hear you."

Pulling my hand down, he kisses my fingertips. "How do you feel about it? I know we didn't..." And shockingly, his cheeks pinken despite his dark complexion. "I just want to make sure we're okay, that you aren't upset or disappointed."

Leaning close, I press my lips to his cheek. "I am definitely not disappointed. I'm so lucky to have you."

"Not again." I hear Wyck's groan from the back.

I turn quickly, trying to hide my panic that he might have overheard our conversation. His hair is sticking up all over his head, and there are dark circles under his eyes. The strain of the last couple of days is beginning to show.

I turn around and give him an embarrassed smile. The look he gives back is anything but embarrassed or smiling for that matter. His navy eyes are harsh as they lock onto mine, guarded and a little frightening. His jaw is tense as he runs his hand through his hair. Feeling naked, as though he can see everything Easton and I did in that room with his piercing stare, I'm the first to break eye contact. I reach out to his mind to see if I can hear his thoughts, and sure enough, he's sending me a message loud and clear—not words, just frustration. My stomach churns. Despite all that's happened and maybe because of it, Wyck is my friend, and I can't stand his feeling betrayed. I have to find a way around this situation with him.

"Turn left in 100 feet," says the robotic voice of the GPS.

"What the hell?" Easton says. Even though we haven't met a car in ages, he switches on his blinker as he turns onto the gravel road.

Dread creeps over me as I turn my attention to the landscape, and I know it isn't the late-afternoon sun creating the sweat trickle that slides down my spine. Trees canopy the rough road, and the eerie shadows cause a chill that has nothing to do with temperature. Foreboding breathes a warning in my ear, my palm immediately responding.

Whether catching my dread or from a sense of his own, Easton reaches back and shakes Coop's still-sleeping form. "Wake up, man." His calm voice belies the vibes his brain's blasting into mine.

Cooper blinks rapidly and grunts as he shifts his big body around to sit up, dragging poor Abby along with him. "What's up? You need a break?" he asks, his voice gravelly from disuse. Stretching his arms over his head so that his fingertips brush the headliner, he twists his neck to one side then the other, popping it loudly.

"No, Coop. Look outside." Easton lifts his chin toward the windshield.

"What is it?" Abby asks, stretching and straightening as Cooper leans toward the window on his left as though getting closer to it might change the scenery.

The gloom thickens with the trees as we drive farther down the road. Like some forgotten path from a Hawthorne novel, the road actually narrows so that some of the branches brush the sides of the SUV as though trying to yank us forcibly from the safety inside.

Easton glances at Wyck in the rearview mirror. "Wyck, got any idea where this road's taking us?" But Wyck silently shakes his head without meeting Easton's eyes. Once again I reach out, but this time I speak to his mind, watching him in the mirror when Easton turns his attention back to the road.

Talk to me, Wyck. What do you think this means?

His response is immediate though he never lifts his gaze to mine in the mirror, stonily staring out at the forest surrounding us.

Nothing good. No way my mom's living back here. She's scared of everything—insects, animals. Didn't even want us camping. No way she's living in this creep show voluntarily.

The implications of his last statement finally force his eyes to mine in the mirror.

We'll find out together.

He nods once before dropping his eyes to his lap as tension and downright fear seeps from him into me.

"Destination ahead on right," chirps the mechanical GPS voice, totally oblivious to the fear of the passengers or the strange location it has directed us to.

All heads swivel as one to the right where a twisted iron gate, once probably proud and shining, highlights the dread we've all been feeling. In large, rusty lettering across a banner-style arch, the words Holy Oaks Cemetery glower out at us. Weeds of brown and green choke the entrance like they're trying to keep out the intrusion of visitors, and if I had my choice, I would gladly let them.

"Shit," Coop mutters.

Exactly. I turn fully around in my seat and face Wyck's withered face as he gapes at the dilapidated entrance. "Wyck," I say, trying to draw his gaze to mine, but he maintains his stare. "Wyck," I say louder.

When he doesn't respond the second time, I begin climbing between and over seats to reach him in the back. I plop into the seat beside him, but not until I touch his hand does he finally turn to me. His expression stabs into my memory, taking me back to the time right after Aunt Charlotte was killed. It's the same one I saw every time I looked in the mirror.

"Wyck, is there *any* way you got the wrong address?" I ask, praying for a glimmer of hope.

When he shakes his head slowly, I know we have only one choice.

CHAPTER ELEVEN

THE CHOKING GRASS and brambles catch on the hem of my jeans as I walk through the gate, dragging Wyck behind me. Surprisingly, Easton didn't protest when I climbed out of the SUV still holding Wyck's hand, the certainty of what we would find making it clammy. With a quiet head nod, Easton had merely given the keys to Cooper and taken up a position behind Abby, who was more than a little spooked at entering the 'this is the part where they kill us' graveyard.

Glancing around at the headstones, most covered in a green moss or mold of some kind and darkened with age, I have no idea where to start, and then I realize I don't even know Wyck's last name. All these weeks together and I've never asked that simple, fundamental question. Briefly, it registers that I really don't know Wyck at all, but I don't have time to dwell on that right now.

"What's your mother's name?" I ask as gently as possible because he seems as fragile as eggshells.

In a low voice far removed from his usual swagger, he replies, "Joyce. Joyce Anderson."

I turn to make sure everyone heard, and when I get nods from all of them, we begin our search, Easton splitting from Cooper and Abby who isn't budging from Coop's side.

The cemetery's not large, so it doesn't take long before Easton calls out to me and waves Wyck and me over to where he's standing at the edge of the cemetery grounds where it borders the forest. He steps respectfully back and drops his gaze, and I note vaguely that Cooper and Abby are walking toward us.

On a small stone in harsh block lettering and surrounded by brown grass and weeds is the name 'Joyce Anderson,' no dates, no epitaph. The grave is obviously not as old as most of the others here because it is slightly mounded, but this didn't happen recently. Joyce Anderson died shortly after her boys left her.

Wyck kneels, but when I try to pull my hand from his, his grip tightens until I know my fingers must be turning purple. With an unsteady hand, he brushes his fingertips across her name and releases a shaky breath. I grit my teeth hard against the tears that tighten my throat. Even though I didn't get to bury my mother or Aunt Charlotte, I know what he's feeling as surely as if I had invaded his mind. Loss is a universal pain, and if I look at him, I'll fall back into the abyss of it.

"I'm so sorry, Mom," he whispers then he pulls our joined hands against his face, and I crouch down to embrace him. As soon as I do, he yanks me into his arms and buries his head in the crook of my neck where he begins to sob unashamedly. I don't know what else to do, so I tighten my arms around him.

"I did this to her," he mumbles against my neck. "I let them have her. I was her only hope, and I let her die."

"No, Wyck, you can't think like that. You were trying to save her," I whisper, running my hand across his shoulders in that instinctual gesture.

He backs away slightly so that his indigo eyes, magnified by his tears, stare into mine, and his expression hardens. "Save her? Save her? But I didn't, did I, Princess?"

Abruptly, he stands, leaving me kneeling on the ground looking up at him. "I'm so worthless that I couldn't even save myself until you came along." Turning back to his mother's headstone, he tightens his hands into fists at his side, lifts his head, and screams at the twilight sky, his voice more animal than human. His head hanging, his breathing heavy, he mumbles, "What the hell good am I?"

"I've wondered the same thing more than once," a cold voice says from the woods in front of us. Stepping out slowly, Ferguson comes into view, dressed in his black uniform and strapped with two guns and at least one knife. His right eye, the source of his Earth Element, is still covered with a patch, but I very clearly remember the power it unleashes when he removes the covering.

We collectively tense as he starts toward us, limping slightly, but he chuckles humorlessly and motions behind him. From the trees, a young boy with light blond hair and wide eyes appears, dressed in the same uniform minus the weapons. Zeb, the little fire starter. And behind him, moving hesitantly, a beautiful, familiar face, the face of an angel—Griffin.

Wyck's gasp is audible, and he involuntarily steps back as the force of the betrayal hits him. His brother, the brother who refused to leave with us, the brother who knew the truth about their father's death, is at the grave of the mother he claimed was safe. I wonder if he knew all along until I look into his eyes. His eyes tell the story. "Hello, Wyck. I knew you would search for her."

Without looking away from his twin, Wyck reaches for my hand again when I stand. "Griffin, tell me you didn't know. Tell me this is all a sick surprise for you, too."

So caught up in his brother's sudden appearance, Wyck doesn't seem to perceive the danger we are all in, but I do. A tingle begins in my chest and expands throughout my body, culminating in my palm, but I know I'm not at the top of my game. I glance over my shoulder. Easton is motionless, his jaw tight. He obviously remembers Ferguson and is itching to finish what he started that first day in the facility. Cooper has pushed Abby behind him, but I can hear her whimper. I have to protect her. She's the weakest, still not completely back from her long illness. Not knowing what else to do, I reach into her mind.

Abby, when it starts, you run. Don't stop until you get to your car. Get in, and drive away. I can't do this if I think you are in danger again.

This is not the first time I've put a thought into Abby's head, but I feel rather than hear her squeak of shock. Then a timid voice pushes back into my head.

I will. Be careful, V.

I make eye contact with Cooper who tips his head slightly as if to say he understands his job in all this, keeping Abby safe. When I face front again, Griffin has dropped his gaze. Wyck's breathing increases.

"You knew," he says disgustedly. "How long?" Wyck asks, the quiver in his voice mirrored by the tension in his body. When Griffin doesn't answer, Wyck snaps, his face contorting in rage. "How long has she been dead?" He steps toward his brother.

Looking anywhere but at his twin, Griffin shrugs. "A while. I told you what you needed to hear. I was trying to convince you to stay at the facility."

Wyck lunges for Griffin, but I dig my heals into the hard-packed ground and hold him back with the hand that's still in mine, but Wyck is too determined, and he begins to drag me with him while Griffin, eyes fearful, steps back toward the forest. Easton quickly grabs Wyck around the chest, pulling him back against himself to keep Wyck from advancing. Despite his struggles, Wyck cannot break free of Easton's hold.

"Let me go!" Wyck yells, eyes blazing.

Ferguson smiles evilly and steps between the brothers, daring Wyck to make a move. "I've been given orders not to hurt you," he says, pointing at Wyck then at me, "or you. But nobody said anything about the others." He pulls a gun from his holster. "So, unless you wanna leave one of your friends here, I suggest you calm down." He looks around as though he's just realized where he is. "Fitting actually. They can join the rest of these wastes of space." He smiles again as he props his foot on Joyce's headstone.

Inhaling sharply, Wyck resumes his struggles, redoubles his efforts, and this time Easton has to dig in his heels to hold Wyck back. But before he can escape, Griffin steps close to Ferguson, right in front of his brother.

"Wyck, stop this please." His pleading eyes meet Wyck's. "She wouldn't leave us alone. Commander Matthews tried to save her, did save her when they had to... when dad refused to let us join. But she wouldn't stop. She weaseled her way into the facility. She looked insane when I saw—" He stops, his eyes wide with panic at what he just unintentionally revealed.

Judging by Wyck's expression and the straightening of his shoulders, he knows exactly what Griffin was about to say but asks anyway. "When you saw what?" I can feel his hand shaking with his restrain. Griffin swallows hard but doesn't continue. "You saw her? You saw her at the facility!" Wyck yells.

"Yes, Wyck, I saw her several months ago."

Easton and I exchange shocked expressions and release Wyck.

CHAPTER TWELVE

WITH A SAVAGE GROWL, Wyck charges Griffin, jumping lithely over his mother's short tombstone and clipping Ferguson in the shoulder to reach Griffin. Wyck and Griffin crash to the ground, a tangle of arms and legs. Ferguson grabs for Wyck, but Easton tackles him. Zeb, eyes popping like a cracked-out Pekinese, raises his palm, and although I know I'm no match for him at the moment, I raise my hand. A bluff goes a long way.

"Don't even think it," I say, using every ounce of my strength to turn my hand into a blue spotlight. I don't need to read his thoughts to tell he's remembering our last encounter when we retrieved him from the juvenile facility where he'd been placed on suspicion of killing his parents.

Glancing over my shoulder, I see Abby running toward the exit, keys dangling from her hand. Cooper, his long legs eating up the distance between Easton and him, lurches toward the grappling pair. Ferguson catches Easton with a right to the mid-section, and Easton crumples like a soda can.

"Cooper, don't let him uncover his eye!" I yell. Cooper dives and wraps his arms around Ferguson's chest, pinning his arms and hands to his sides, but Ferguson kicks out, catching Easton in the shoulder as Easton tries to rise.

"How could you? How could you let them do this, Griffin?" Wyck has flipped Griffin to his back and is punching him in the face. With each punch, blood spews from his mouth and spatters on Wyck's white t-shirt. I have to stop this before he kills Griffin, but when I rush forward to pull them apart, Zeb seizes his chance. His palm shoots out and a stream of bright, orange flame leaps onto the dead grass between the two of us. Fire hops from grave to grave until Wyck and I are separated from Easton and Cooper by a three-foot high wall of heat. Zeb rushes toward the safety of the woods without looking back. As I watch his retreating form, a part of me actually feels sorry for this kid who's found himself in the middle of a fight that's not his own, but that part doesn't stop me from sending a blast directly at his ass, knocking him face first in the ground.

A wave of dizziness rocks my head, and my knees slump forward as though they've lost their connection with the rest of me. Momentarily dazed, I see the whole thing in slow motion—Easton and Coop wrestling with Ferguson, Ferguson kicking and thrashing wildly, Fireboy flat on his stomach eating dirt fifty feet away, and Wyck screaming wordlessly now while ruthlessly shaking Griffin's still form.

"Vivian!" Easton's voice cuts across the fire as our gazes meet. Releasing his hold on Ferguson, he swings in my direction. I see Ferguson smile through blood-coated teeth. He viciously elbows Coop in the chest. When Coop falls backward onto the ground, Ferguson stands triumphantly and lifts his hand to his eye patch.

The ground begins to rumble, and through unfocused eyes, I see the trees shake as though protesting the unnatural event taking place around them. Reaching out hands as unsteady as the shifting earth beneath me, I will my body to stay upright, but my head is sagging forward, too tired to resist much longer.

"Wyck!" Easton again, only this time his voice sounds distant, like he's yelling at me from the end of a long tunnel. "Get Vivian!"

Right before I hit the quaking ground, strong arms wrap around me and hold me close, my head finally giving up the fight and sinking onto a solid chest. Wyck struggles to stand, but the shaking is just too fierce, and he's forced to his knees again. A fissure about the width of my hand opens near my leg, and as dirt waterfalls over the side, my fuzzy brain registers that we'll be joining it soon.

Forcing my head back so that I can see Wyck's face, I mumble, "Wyck, you have to stop him."

His panicked eyes peer into mine. "I can't! We don't know if it'll work on Ferguson!"

"You have to try," I whisper without knowing if he can even hear me over the thunderous rumbling. Cracks surround us now, creating a shrinking island of ground for the two of us.

His chest rises on a deep inhale as he shouts, "Stop!"

Instantly, the ground stills beneath us.

"It… it worked. I can't believe! Let's go!" Wyck lurches to his feet with me clutched to his chest. When he swings us around, I see that even the fire has been extinguished.

"What the hell just happened?" Cooper, eyes as large as his meaty hands, asks from his position on the ground.

Easton rises and reaches for me as Wyck jumps a fissure.

"I've got her. Don't waste time. I don't know how long the effects will last," Wyck says, his expression brokering no argument. "And cover his eye!" he tosses over his shoulder as he rushes us away.

I glance around his arm just in time to see Cooper nail a statuesque Ferguson with a hard right to his jaw before slipping the eye patch back in place.

CHAPTER THIRTEEN

WHEN WE REACH THE SUV, Wyck sets me on my feet just long enough to whip open the cargo door. I lean heavily on his side, my hands gripping his shirt to keep from collapsing. He lifts me inside and follows me in, wrenching down the door. A choking fear overwhelms me. All I've ever wanted was to be a normal girl, but now that my power has jumped ship and left me adrift, I'm looking for a lifeboat that's already sailed. This weakness is bad — very bad.

"Start the car, Abby!" he yells toward the driver's seat where Abby nods quickly and cranks the engine. I hear Cooper and Easton jerk open doors and feel the shake of the vehicle as they launch themselves inside.

"Drive!" Easton screams as he crawls over the seats to reach us in the back.

Gravel flies as Abby spins the tires and whips the wheel into a U-turn, sending us flying back the way we came.

Easton's beautiful face, brows drawn tight together, appears over the top of the seat. "Vivian, what happened to you?" He leans over and grabs my hand.

"I'm so tired, Easton." I try to keep meeting his eyes, but I can't hold mine open.

"Vivian, Vivian!" Easton's voice fades as I stop trying.

* * *

"I don't know. Just keep driving till we get to a motel." Wyck's deep voice resonates against my ear. When I open my eyes, everything is dark, and I have a moment of freak out thinking I've gone blind as well as lost my Gift until I realize it's night. As my eyes adjust, I look up into Wyck's eyes.

"Hey, you're back," he says, smiling sadly.

I put my hand against his chest and gingerly pull away from him as the world spins slightly. When I'm able to focus again, I stare at the blood splattered like angry paint on Wyck's shirt beneath my hand. The fight, the fire, and our escape rushes back like a bad dream. Remembering the cemetery is a shot of cold water, and I jolt back against the side of the cargo area, bumping my head on the window.

The sudden movement draws Easton's attention, and he slides down his seat toward me, reaching over to grasp my shoulder. "You okay? Damn, babe, what happened to you back there?"

"Is she awake?" Abby calls from her post in the driver's seat, trying to adjust the rearview mirror so that she can see us.

"You watch the road!" Cooper exclaims, grabbing the wheel as Abby jerks the SUV to the right.

"I—wow!" I drop my head into my hands as a throbbing pain that has nothing to do with smacking the window sets up a hateful tattoo.

Wyck scoots closer. "What is it?"

"My head," I reply, rubbing my temples.

He takes my hand. "Try to light this up," he commands.

I concentrate even though the little drummer boy in my head is playing a percussion solo but nothing, nada, not even a sparkle.

"That's what I thought. Princess, your batteries are dead." He smirks at his joke, his full lips quirking up at one corner.

Leaning back on the window I assaulted with my skull a few minutes ago, I glance over at Easton, his lips tight with tension. As a fresh wave of pain hits me, I wince and so does Easton.

"What would help?" he asks.

"Talk louder, you three! I can't hear you up here!" Abby yells, again yanking the wheel in her distraction.

Cooper groans. "Pull over. I'm drivin'."

"No, you drive all the time," Abby grumps as the two begin an impassioned discussion on who's a better driver.

"I'll be fine." It's a lie, but I know that Easton will only worry if I tell him my brain is using a jackhammer in an escape attempt. "Where are we?"

He sighs, lowering his brows as though he has mind-reading abilities or maybe a bull crap detector. "I don't know. As soon as we get to a town, we're stopping for the night."

"So, what happened?" I ask, using my palm to massage my forehead.

Wyck shrugs. "Nothing. Abby peeled us out of there, and we've been driving for about an hour." He pulls his long legs in tight and drapes one arm over his raised knee.

"You used your power." I squint over at him, and he only shrugs again.

"Yeah, guess I did." He shifts uncomfortably as though he doesn't want to talk about it, and who would? He beat his twin to a mangled pulp after discovering his mother is dead and buried in a cemetery so far off the beaten path that he'll probably never be able to return to it.

"Don't get me wrong, I'm really glad it worked, but how? How were you able to freeze Ferguson? We weren't sure the Twister thing wouldn't work on the Gifted." I remember the conversation Griffin and I had in the training area of the facility. Griffin explained to me that I could remember the before and after of his 'undo' ability because I am Gifted. 'Normals' only remember the after. That's how I knew Wallis was more than he let on. Thinking of Wallis, his kindness and his sacrifice to save me, tears at my heart the way this headache is tearing at my head, and I push away the thought for the moment.

"I didn't think it would." He shakes his head and looks down at Griffin's blood, polka dotting his white shirt like a macabre fashion statement. "I thought... I was always told—" When he lifts his eyes to mine, I see the navy fire burning there even in the dim interior of the SUV. "He knew all along. He knew what I was going to be, and he told me that it wouldn't work because—"

"He didn't want you trying to use it against him." I finish for him.

"Who? What are we talking about?" Easton's watching the conversation like a tennis match, swiveling his head between the two of us with his brows drawn together in confusion.

"Matthews. He told me that none of the Twister powers would work on the Gifted, and he used Griffin's as an example," Wyck answers through gritted teeth. "Why did I not realize this sooner? Griffin was able to reverse stabbing Lilah on the plane, so it obviously does work, but Matthews said that I probably wouldn't have the same ability as Griffin, so I just assumed... I've been so stupid." He grasps his hair in a tug.

"Don't beat yourself up over it. He's a master manipulator, remember?"

"Wait, what do you mean?" Easton asks.

"Griffin attacked Lilah, stabbed her in the chest with a knife, on the way to retrieve that Zeb kid. He was taking up for me." Wyck's expression softens as he drops his gaze again to the front of his shirt, but when he looks up, his eyes harden. "He reversed it, but we all remember it happening. If we were Normals, we wouldn't have remembered the attack. It would have been like it never happened. Only Griffin would know. He should have left that knife in her chest," Wyck says, leaning back on the far side of the cargo area.

I purse my lips and nod my head which has settled to a dull throb, like the seven dwarfs are mining away at a chain-gang pace.

Wyck glances out at the darkness, seeing only our reflections. "Wonder why she wasn't with them at my mom's... at the cemetery?" I can feel the grief pouring out of Wyck despite having no power at present. I guess you don't need a special gift to feel the pain of your friend.

My mind flashes to the look of undiluted misery, the mental snapshot of pure grief on Wyck's face as he'd stared at his mother's tombstone, reached out to touch her name as if he needed that affirmation to realize the truth. I think of my own mom, no tombstone and no grave. Besides Aunt Charlotte and me, did anyone else mourn her? Would someone besides us (like, oh say, my dad!) have knelt at her grave in dejection, missing her, loving her even though she was gone?

To distract myself from my own haze of unhappiness but before I can initiate the intelligent half of my brain, I blurt out, "Lilah's helping Hoyt." In unison, both sets of male eyes spear me.

"How do you know that?" Easton's suspicious gaze is enough to spike the river dance of agony in my head.

Damn! Did I really just tell on myself? Being drained is affecting my judgment. "Uh... I... well... that is" —I sigh— "I saw her, okay?"

"You saw her?" Wyck's glaring at me as he leans in closer. "What does that mean, Princess?"

Cooper's voice booms from the front of the SUV. "Do we need to pull over for this explosion?"

"Funny, Coop." I roll my eyes. "When we were still at the Shady Rest, she appeared." I wave my hands around like I'm going to pull a rabbit from a hat at an eight year old's party. "Somehow, Hoyt had channeled her abilities to find me and sent her as the messenger."

"What did he say?" Easton asks.

"Same ol' thing. Return to him to save you guys. Thing is, he's still too weak to come after me—us—or he would have appeared himself in the flesh, not a vision version."

"Why didn't those three take us back this afternoon?" Cooper asks, turning back to look at us.

"My guess is that wasn't what that pleasant encounter was about," Wyck replies. "That was about showing us the extent of their control. I mean, they killed my parents, brainwashed my brother, and ambushed us easily. Matthews wants us to run scared of his ability, and when he's strong enough..."

He doesn't finish, but then he doesn't have to. We all know what will happen when he is at full strength again. He'll come gunning with a passion. We not only made him physically weak, but we also rattled his ego, his precious sense of control. Even if I agreed to go back, my life with the Liaisons would be hell. He would see to that as punishment and a permanent reminder of his tyrant status.

"Now, the important question. Why didn't you tell us?" Wyck asks. He tilts his head as his lips thin in a grim line while he waits for my answer.

"I have a good reason," I begin, which I will give you as soon as I come up with it, I mentally add.

After a long stretch of tense staring from both of them, I sigh. "I got nothing here." I blame the headache.

Wyck throws up his hands as he pulls himself over the back of the seat where Easton's sitting. "You deal with her. I need a break from babysitting," he grumbles as he continues to climb over seats to get as far from me as possible. When he's sitting right behind Cooper, he slams down forcefully and crosses his arms over his chest.

As I gape open-mouthed, Easton raises his eyebrows and looks toward the seat where Wyck is now sitting. "Think he's got the right idea," he says, crawling his way to the front as well. Easton is agreeing with Wyck, I'm powerless, and my head's going to explode. The world is definitely out of balance tonight.

So, left alone with my bad decision, I draw my knees up, rest my head on my folded arms, and listen to the techno-beat hammering in my head, wishing I hadn't just pissed off my two dance partners.

CHAPTER FOURTEEN

Wishing

Head thrown back,
cascade of chocolate curls
rippling down her slim, bare back,
her laughter at his fall from the bank
makes me wish he would slip again.
He followed my suggestion,
brought her to our lake.
I knew she would love it.
Even now, watching them,
spying from afar,
I wish I could have been
the one.
When he sloshes from the water,
she gifts him with a smile,
touches his cheek,
a whisper of her cool fingertips.
I have never seen him so
happy,
not since we were boys,
before wars,
and collections,

and service to the cause.
Now jealousy rides my shoulders
like a twisted joke.
Me.
Jealous of this assignment,
this love he thinks he's found.
A part of me wishes
I could give him
his happily ever after.
A part of me wishes
I could be him in this moment—
a larger part than I care to admit
even to myself.
He removes the oversized hat
protecting that creamy skin
of her pert nose
from the greed of the late afternoon sun.
He's swimming in the silvery pools
of her eyes,
eyes I've only seen through dark lenses,
his mind, so open and free,
no idea I'm nearby.
Wet lips meet cool, giggling ones,
and a jolt races along my senses.
For one brief sigh of time,
I am kissing her.
Her peace and contentment
belong to me.
Her flirtatious spirit
longs for me.
Her breathy exhales
tickle my skin.
Her yearning, her desire
are mine.
But I pull from his mind long before
he pulls away from her.
Every minute, I risk his discovery,

then his questions,
then his fury
once again.
I cannot afford to lose his trust.
I cannot afford to lose him.
They will punish him if he fails,
and I,
I will be forced to punish
them.

CHAPTER FIFTEEN

SPARKLING BLUE RINGED IN GREEN. A lake. Warm sun on my wet bathing suit, drying my hair. Wind licking drops from my arms, my legs, my face. Drowsy eyes, then his voice. "Thought you might like this," he says. Purple petals, slender stem, the smell of summer. I smile up at him, feeling so loved... so safe. I try to focus on his blurry face, try so hard to figure out who this is making me feel what I don't understand, but his image is a vortex that spins away from me. Then the feeling is gone, and I am cold.

No sun, no warmth, no lake—only fog that chills. I wrap my arms around myself, but I can't stop the shaking. Fear, fear and confusion. I reach out, for what I don't know, but there is only nothingness. There is someone here, but it's not him. Someone familiar but not safe. The fog thins, and I'm looking at eyes, closed eyes with no face beneath. When I reach out, the eyes flip open in shock. Black eyes silently scream.

* * *

I jump, sweat coating my neck and back, and I can't breathe. It's too dark, too dark in this room, black like the eyes. I drag in breath after breath without success, like there is a hole between my gaping mouth and my lungs. Dizziness engulfs me as my head swims. There is no air in this room. Panic leaps into my dry throat. Swinging my legs to the side, I stumble to the doorway, clutching the frame. I have to get air; I have to get outside. But where is that? I fumble with the door knob, tingling hands making sloppy work of opening it.

Another room, moonlight through a window to my left, lighting the way to another door, but this one is open. Voices drift from outside. Black spots dance in front of my eyes. My oxygen-starved brain flashes a warning of lights out. I stagger to the door, flinging open the unlatched screen seconds before my legs give up as I sink to my knees.

Air, sweet with a sting of wood smoke. I gulp it in and let my head fall forward to my trembling hand, rough wood beneath my other hand where I brace myself to keep from falling over as the spots recede. For a minute, my confused senses tell me I'm home, the home I shared with Aunt Charlotte, my only real home. I'm on our porch, and she is beside me, but when I look there is no one.

The dream of the lake. I was home in the dream. My home. But how is that possible? The only lake near our house was miles away. My brain works swiftly to process. Maybe it was just one of those strange dreamscapes where you think you're one place, but you're not. Then I realize it was the man, not the lake, which felt like home. It was him, the man whose face I couldn't see, the man whose voice I've heard before somehow. But the images of warmth and security fade and are replaced by black eyes. I know those eyes, too.

"V!" Abby's blonde hair, shining with the light of the full moon, fills my vision. Jerking me upright, she runs her hands over my face and arms, searching for a sign of injury. "What happened? Did you fall?" When I only stare at her, she sputters nervously. "Well, duh! That's obvious, huh? Did you, like, trip? Are you hurt? Easton!" she yells, loudly and kind of in my face. "Oh, sorry! I'm totally screwing this up," she mutters, pulling me forcefully to my feet despite her petite frame. When I weave slightly, she grabs me hard around the waist and wraps my arm around her neck.

"Oh, no you don't! No falling on nurse Abby's watch!" She drag-lifts me to the first of three short steps down from the porch and plops me on my butt, momentarily releasing all that precious oxygen I just managed to force in my lungs.

At my grunt, she smiles sheepishly again, "Sorry again, V." She leans me against the post to my right, both hands hovering near my shoulders until she's sure I'm stable. "Stay here," she commands as she jogs to the corner of the porch, mumbling, "Dang men! Don't they hear me?" She leans around, keeping an eye on me while yelling, "Easton, get your butt up here!"

Glancing around while I catch my breath again, I see a huge oak tree near a gravel road about ten feet from the porch steps. Where are we? Pounding feet arrive from my right, and Easton, Wyck, and Cooper are all staring at me questioningly.

"She was on the porch when I came around to get the hot dogs, like *on* the porch, on her knees." Abby moves her hands all around, marionette-style.

"How do you feel, babe?" Easton leans down until we're eye level and rests his hand on my shoulder. "You fell asleep in the back. You've been asleep awhile."

"Yeah, V, we couldn't even get you to wake up when we got here, so we put you in the bedroom," Abby says, nodding her head.

"Where exactly is here?" I look over my shoulder at the small porch, the screen door, the clothesline strung between porch posts.

"We rented this cabin," Cooper answers. "Got it cheap because the plumbing's not workin' right." He looks so pleased with himself, his chest puffed out as he puts his arm around Abby's shoulders.

"The plumbing, the stove, the air conditioner," she grumps, deflating his pride like a hole in a balloon. I can practically hear it hissing out.

"It's a little" —he pauses, slowly shaking his head and waving his hand— "rustic, sunshine, and maybe kinda small with only the one bedroom, but it'll work for a day or two. We drove for about an hour after you woke up." He clears his throat and glances at Wyck who is standing slightly behind the others with his head down. "We stopped at a motel down the road, but they were full. The owner said he could rent us this place if we were desperate, which we *are*." Coop stares pointedly at Abby. "We all need to rest up for a while, and this place is as good as any." When she rolls her eyes, he rubs her back. "It's like camping, sunshine."

Great. I hate camping. "How much like camping, Coop?" I ask, thinking of bugs and snakes and poison ivy on my... yeah, but that was just the one time when I was ten and way too adventurous, trying to be all Lewis and Clark.

"Well, we have runnin' water." Abby interrupts him.

"In the sink, not the shower and not the toilet," she says arching one eyebrow.

"We got a whole bunch of woods out back and a lake a quarter mile away!" Coop exclaims, holding up his hands in frustration. "It's not like we're livin' here forever, Abby. It's just for a day or two. Go get the hot dogs, girl, and quit your complainin'." He grins and swats her on the behind.

She grabs her butt, gasping open-mouthed, then she giggles and all but floats into the cabin.

Easton grins lopsidedly, his perfect profile illuminated in the moonlight, but he grows serious when he peers back at me. "You okay?"

"Yeah." Another lie. I don't want to tell Easton about the dreams right this second. Now that I'm awake, breathing, and surrounded by people who care about me, it seems silly to dwell on dreams, even dreams that felt so real, especially dreams that felt so real.

"Come on, Wyck," Cooper says, clapping him on the back. "Let's go find some proper sticks for roastin' those dogs."

Wyck, who's been uncharacteristically quiet for this entire exchange, nods and begins to follow Cooper back around the house.

"No wait, Wyck. I need to talk to you." Automatically, I reach out for his hand to stop him. Easton stiffens beside me but to his credit, he doesn't say a word.

He shrugs and sits beside me on the step. "Sure," he says and smiles, but it doesn't reach his eyes.

I speak into Easton's mind.

I just want to check on him, okay?

Easton gives me the faintest of nods.

He's lucky to have you, babe.

"Guess it's you and me, buddy," Easton says. "Let's go find those sticks. I'm starving." He squeezes my shoulder and kisses my cheek.

Cooper nods. "We gotta find the perfect sticks."

Abby reemerges from the cabin, a package of hot dogs and buns in hand. "Perfect sticks, huh?" she asks.

Cooper holds out his hand to help her step down from the porch. "Yes, sunshine," he replies as all three of them walk around the side of the cabin. "You don't want your dog fallin' off. It's all fun and games till somebody burns their weeny."

Easton groans; Abby giggles then I'm left alone with Wyck, who's shaking his head. I smile, but when he looks at me, the sadness in his face wipes away Coop's humor. "So, how are you?" I ask.

"Humph" — he snorts — "how am I?" He seems to be asking himself rather than repeating my question. "Dead father, dead mother, and a brother that's as good as dead to me." He nods as though he's just then made up his mind. "Yeah, that pretty much sums it up."

I grip his hand tightly, wishing I could take away his pain.

"The worst part about all this," he says, leaning against the opposite post, "I've lost my entire family." He glances away, but in the bright moonlight I still see the tears pool in his eyes.

Grabbing his other hand, I pull him into my arms. For a minute he doesn't respond then he wraps his arms around me and drops his head to my shoulder. "Wyck, you can be my family any day." I feel rather than hear his sigh.

He pulls away and resumes his position holding up the porch. "I'm sorry, Princess. Here I am bemoaning my fate when you've gone through pretty much the same thing—lost your mom, lost your home, betrayed by family."

"It's okay, Wyck. Say what you need to say. Let yourself mourn, but don't forget you still have people who care about you."

He snorts unhappily again. "You're the only one who gives a shit about me."

"That's not true." I shake my head. "We all care." He raises his brows nearly into his shaggy hair. "Don't look at me like that. It's true. Me, Cooper, Abby, even Easton, we all care about you."

"Easton? Doubtful, Vivian." He smirks with real humor then smiles. "I've never met a girl like you before. I actually think I care about you, Princess."

My turn to snort. "Gee, thanks. You really know how to make a girl feel special," I say, batting my eyelashes like a 1950s vixen.

He laughs. "Let's go eat a hot dog." He pulls me to my feet, but when I sway a little, he grabs me and positions me right back on the step. "What are you not telling me?" His voice and face are heavy with concern.

Taking a deep breath and letting it out slowly, I shrug. "I had a dream, dreams actually, two, and I woke up hyperventilating and freaking out. Guess I'm still a little shaky."

"What kind of dreams?" he asks, not finding my revelation at all weird. But I suppose when you're both members of a never-ending sideshow, nothing's unusual.

I inhale and look away. "Well, one was really good, comforting. I was beside a big lake. I think I'd just gotten out of the water. My suit was damp, my hair dripping. A man—I couldn't see his face—brought me a flower, told me he thought I'd like it." I peer into Wyck's eyes, willing him to understand how significant the dream felt to me. "I was safe and loved."

He nods. "Think it was Easton? The man in your dream?"

"No, his voice was familiar, like I know him—" I pause as another image returns in a rush, an image of a bed and early-morning sunlight through a window.

"What is it?" Wyck takes my hand again.

"This isn't my first dream of him. I just realized. I recognize his voice because I've heard it before in another dream. Before we found your mom, I dreamed about a room with white curtains and a soft quilt and a man waking me up. He called out to me. What do you think this means?"

He sighs and shakes his head, his eyes looking away as though he's searching the darkness for an answer. "Could be nothing, a random guy in your dreams. Is he young or old? Are you in love with him?"

"No, it's not that kind of feeling. I feel connected to him but not in a romantic way."

"Could he be a representation of family? Like what you wish your home was like?" he asks, motioning with our joined hands. It should feel wrong to hold hands with another boy, but Wyck and I've been through a lot. Besides, it makes me feel good to connect with him like this.

"Maybe, guess he could be anything really." I watch an ant crawl across the step beside me. "It's just so real, you know? Like... a..."

"Like a vision?" He finishes for me.

"Yeah, like with Mr. Lewis from before, but different." I pick at the flaking paint of the porch.

"You said dreams. What was the other? Because as exciting as lakes and flowers are, I'm thinking that was not what had you hyperventilating." He pegs me with his intense gaze.

I shrug, not wanting to talk about it now that I'm being confronted.

"No, no, no," he says shaking his head. "Uh-uh, you aren't getting out of this, so spill, Princess."

"Okay." I sigh again. "Fog, cold, someone out in the fog, and eyes, black eyes, Wyck."

He jumps to his feet, releasing my hand and pacing in front of the small porch. "Matthews. You dreamed of Matthews?" At my nod, he continues heatedly. "Was it a dream, Vivian, or was it a vision? We have to be sure which one it was."

"I don't know." I run my hands through my hair and, to my horror, I tear up. "I think he was as shocked to see me as I was to see him." I swipe at a lone tear that slips down my cheek. "I think it was real." Looking up at him, I confess. "I think I contacted him."

CHAPTER SIXTEEN

AT THE IMMEDIATE PANIC ON WYCK'S FACE, I jump from the step and begin to pace as though the movement will somehow erase what I've done.

"Not on purpose, obviously! I don't know how it happened. One minute I'm starring in a Lifetime movie complete with flowers, and the next, I'm giving the boogeyman an eye exam!"

"Okay." Wyck, Mr. Logic and Reason, puts out his hands to stop my frantic excuses. "Let's think this through. You had a great dream, a warm and fuzzy dream, then a nightmare about Matthews. Why?"

Confusion twists my features. "Which why?" He raises his brows like I've sprouted a dunce cap from the top of my head. "Why did I have a great dream, or why did I have a nightmare?"

He closes his eyes and shakes his head in a 'God give me patience' gesture. "Why did you have the two dreams back-to-back? There must be a connection."

A connection between my mystery man and the center of evil in the universe? How is that even possible? The feelings were so opposite, from inviting to forbidding. I glance over at Wyck who is giving me his soul-searching stare, running his hand through his hair, and I'm taken back to my room at the facility the night he changed everything I know about my family when he explained what he learned from my confidential files—the night he explained...

"Not two men, Wyck, two brothers," I whisper. "I dreamed about my uncle—"

"And your dad," Wyck finishes my statement.

"Yeah." I sit down next to him. "I was at a lake with my dad."

"So was this a memory from the past or just something you wish would happen?" His brows draw together.

"I don't know. I don't even know how old I was when he and my mom split. I don't remember ever seeing him. How do I know if he saw me at all?" I throw up my hands.

"I don't have an answer, Princess, but something prompted you to connect with Matthews after that dream about your dad." He purses his lips before leaping to his feet to pace again. He suddenly snaps his fingers and turns to me. "Matthews knows where your father is. He's probably the *only* person who knows."

I nod and roll my eyes. "Yeah, we've already established all this, but I wasn't able to get that location, remember? You pulled us apart before I could."

"I pulled you apart because you were mind melting, *remember*?" he sneers, mocking me. "But that's not what I'm getting at. If you connected to him once, you can do it again, and the next time you can get the location from him."

We stare at each other. "Say something."

But I can't say what I want to say. I can't tell him I'm afraid. He's just had a beat down with his brother and saved us all from Ferguson. I can't admit that I'm a coward, too scared to enter that heart of darkness again. What if I can't get out?

Instead, I ask, "What if he uses our connection to find us all?" I know it's a lame excuse that he's too smart to fall for. No way he's letting me off the hook with that one.

"Hello! He already knows! Lilah's little envoy proved that." When I drop my eyes, he squats down on his haunches, forcing me to look at him. "Hey, what's really going on in here?" he asks, using his index finger to rub a tiny circle on my left temple. "Tell me."

"I'm afraid, okay? I know it's stupid, but I can't help it! The thought of going back into his brain scares the hell out of me." I sigh.

He smiles. "I'll be there with you. I'll pull the plug again if need be." When I don't reply, he touches my cheek. "Maybe we can find a way to go through my head. What do you think? Kind of like an insulator. I'll be the middleman, and you won't have to connect with him directly."

He looks so optimistic that I hate to burst his bubble. "I'm afraid that won't work, Wyck. It's hard to explain, and I don't even know how I know this, but you haven't had enough of a mental connection to him to make it work. He's been in your head but not for long enough to make this work."

"*He* hasn't, but *I* have." Easton walks around the corner again. Wyck leaps to his feet and moves back a few feet as though he was doing more than comforting me with an innocent touch.

"Easton, were you eavesdropping?" I ask, watching him walk toward us through narrow eyes.

He scrubs his hand sheepishly across the back of his neck and grins guiltily. "Yeah," he says then adds quickly, "but not on purpose! I was coming to see if you two wanted a hot dog before Cooper eats them all or Abby loses another one in the fire." He drops down beside me on the step. "Sorry."

"It's okay." I touch his knee. "I was going to tell you about the dreams later. Wyck and I were just trying to figure it all out first." He winces like I've stabbed his ego. "I mean, well, I..."

"It's okay, babe," Easton says, mimicking my earlier statement. "I get it, and I'm not mad about it. I promised you I'd try to get along with him." He motions to Wyck, who shrugs nervously.

"So, you think you can help us out here, man?" Wyck asks awkwardly. It feels forced, like having your shoes on the wrong feet, but at least they aren't at each other's throats. I realize suddenly that Wyck didn't take the opportunity to goad Easton when Easton walked around the corner. It would have been his chance to say something incredibly sleazy, but instead, he'd moved away. Maybe this afternoon showed them both were on the same side.

"Yeah, remember the dream?" He peers into my eyes with his aqua stare. "The one where we were together at your old house?" When I nod, he continues. "Hoyt told us he'd been using me to find you and to give you those visions of Mr. Lewis." He takes a deep breath. "Use me to connect with him. Me and that little doohickey Carter made."

"Easton, no, we aren't doing that." He starts to shake his head, but I stand and move right in front of him. "It's too dangerous."

"But you'd let him do it, wouldn't you?" He points to Wyck, sighs and reaches for my shoulders, pulling us close together. "I want to do it. Let me do this for us, for all of us." He gestures to Wyck. "It's my chance to actually do something, to help you for a change." He grins. "When I'm done, you can reward me like a real hero."

I glance back at Wyck who shrugs again. "What's the worst that can happen?" he asks. "You fry his brain, and we'll leave him here with the other junk that doesn't work right. Our only problem will be deciding if you really scrambled his egg or if that's just his normal lack of brain function." He smirks at Easton, who glares. Maybe they aren't quite on the same side yet.

"Go eat a hot dog before I give up trying to be civil to you, jackass."

CHAPTER SEVENTEEN

"ARE YOU SURE ABOUT THIS?" I ask Easton as he settles onto the bed next to me. We're in the cabin's only bedroom and on one of the two beds in the room, he's stretched out, long legs causing his feet to dangle like Christmas ornaments over the end.

Despite all its issues and Abby's griping, the cabin isn't *that* bad. When I stumbled outside earlier, I was too freaked to notice the kitchenette and tiny living room or even the two, full-size beds in the bedroom. Off the bedroom is the thumbnail bathroom with its non-functioning toilet and shower, but everything is tidy and neat though the furniture looks like rejects from a 1970s sitcom—a really bad 1970s sitcom—where the chairs and couch are a strangely complex pattern of greens and oranges. Looks like someone threw up Veg-All all over everything. With the air conditioner out of commission, the only air circulation is coming from a couple of fans, so it's a little like trying to breathe in a closed up car, but it's cheap and quiet. So, it's perfect.

Abby and Cooper have wandered off to the lake, probably to do things that will frighten the fish, and Wyck is waiting in the living room area, close enough in case I have a problem (like broiling the brain of my super-hot boyfriend) but far enough to give us some privacy.

"Let's just get started, babe." He grins, but it doesn't erase the unease from his strained face. "The sooner we get it started, the sooner we can be finished, and I can collect on that reward." He tries to wiggle his brows but stops when I touch his cheek.

"I'm scared, Easton. What if I screw up? What if you end up—"

"What if I don't? What if it works and we get the answers we need?" He rests his hand on mine. "I trust you, Vivian. You should trust yourself."

Taking a deep breath I slip the leather strap of the enhancer Carter designed over my right wrist then the other strap over my middle finger so that the cool metal ring rests center-palm to harness my power, which is stronger but still not completely normal, well as normal as energy shooting out of your hand can be.

"Close your eyes and clear your mind. It will make it easier for me to get inside of your head." I lift my palm to his head as I did to Wyck and to Hoyt in the facility. I brush my fingers through the thick hair above his ear then I too close my eyes and focus on Easton's pulse. He is surprisingly calm considering he could be lobotomized in a matter of minutes.

It's only the work of a couple of seconds to reach into his head. Easton's brain is neat and organized, very methodical. In fact, it's exactly like those holographic computer interfaces in all the big-time Hollywood spy movies or futuristic science fiction shows. Brushing my metaphorical fingers across the surface brings up a screen of files, each clearly labeled with titles like 'school,' 'sports,' or 'family.' He has hundreds of files, and as I sweep my fingers left, another screen of files appears. I'm about to flick past when I notice these files all have a 'V' in front of the file name: 'V home,' 'V school,' 'V tutoring.' All I can do is stare. The entire page of files has the same label, and I think I know what that label means.

Even though I should be hurrying, I can't resist. I tap on a file, and images of me in a shimmery silver gown fill the screen. My auburn hair is swept up with blue orchids resting randomly among the curls. I'm in his car, and I glance over and smile. His thoughts blunder from the memory of prom last spring.

Damn, she's gorgeous! How did we end up going to prom together?

In the memory I reach for his hand.

I'm so glad I suck at English and she got in that fight. I really want to kiss her, like now, right now on the side of the road. But that wouldn't be perfect, and she deserves perfect.

Before I have a chance to 'ohh and ahh,' Easton shifts. He sounds uncomfortable when the real Easton, not the memory one, says,

"Um, babe, can we just stick to connecting with Matthews? There are a few thoughts in there that might embarrass us both."

"Sorry," I murmur, feeling about as high as Abby's enthusiasm at staying here. I draw my hand away, and when he glances into my eyes, I smile. "But thank you, Easton, for reminding me of how much I love you."

Before he can reply, I replace my hand on his temple and dive in again. Without lingering a second time, I make quick work of locating the old connection. Sure enough, buried deep in his subconscious is a little piece of my uncle, lying in wait like a serial killer in the closet.

Opening the connection is easy. Hoyt must have his guard down, but it makes sense because he doesn't really want to find us right now. If he did, Ferguson and company would have been much more successful. They would have brought the whole force to round us up. My visit with Lilah confirms that, too. My uncle is not strong enough to truly challenge me yet. I wonder if he realizes how weak I am as well. Probably not. If he did, I would not be connecting to him through Easton. I would be locked in that facility again, meeting his eyes in person instead of in a dream.

In and out—that's the plan. Get the location and get out, and at first, I think this will be easy. He offers me no resistance. In fact, I think he's sleeping. His mind is surprisingly quiet, peaceful even. I feel his weakness, though.

When I was in junior high I caught the stomach flu, and while I seemed to recover faster than some of my classmates in homeroom, I threw up so much that Aunt Charlotte took me to the doctor, who gave me a shot of that stuff that made me stop puking because it more or less knocked me out. For the entire next day I felt the effects of that shot, a drug-induced sluggishness, sudden movements and loud noises making my heart race. That's the feeling I get from Hoyt's brain, like if I banged on a pan with a wooden spoon he might have a heart attack.

Okay, got to find memories of my father, his twin. Images of two blond boys sitting on the edge of adolescence, scrawny bodies poised to swing from a knotted rope into a lake. Then later, the boys aged a few years, playing cards with clay chips of red, white, and blue, surrounded by soldiers in black uniforms, tossing in cards while one boy grins victoriously. Older now, the shadow of whiskers on once-smooth faces in a severe argument, tempers as hot as the house blazing behind them, and blood, so much blood.

"I'll give you the location."

His voice startles me, and I nearly pull out of Easton's head on reflex alone. "Even in my weakened state, I am mentally stronger than you, and in your weakened state, you are no match. But I must applaud you, my dear, for using the boy." He chuckles. "Perhaps you and I are not so different after all. We know how to benefit from the pain of others."

"I'm not using him." Alarm jumbles my thoughts as I scramble to decide what to do. I will never have this opportunity again. He'll be expecting it and will block Easton from now on. I'm not worried about him locating us since he obviously knows where we are, but if I stay, what will he do to Easton?

He chuckles again. "You have taken over another human being's mind, a weaker human being than yourself, and you are disregarding his reservations to accomplish your own ends. Is that not the case, Vivian?"

"He doesn't have reservations. So, no, you're wrong. He wanted to do this, volunteered to do it."

"Volunteering doesn't take away his fear, and he is afraid, my dear—unquestioningly afraid—yet you use him still. Impressive. But you need not have gone to so much trouble really. If it means that much to you, I'll tell you where your father is."

I snort in derision. "Really?" I ask, mocking him. "Then why not give it to me before, save us the trouble yourself?"

"That other attack on my person wasn't actually about finding your father. It was about power. You needed mine weakened in order to escape."

Maybe he's right. Maybe it was about showing him how powerful I was, scaring him. Finding my dad might have just been the icing on the cake, but right now, that's all semantics. I have to remember my goal, and the longer I stay in Easton's mind, the more dangerous it is for him. "Then give it to me so we can end this meeting." I sound more forceful than I feel.

"What makes you think you can handle finding him? I've already told you that you won't like what you find."

"Yeah, through Lilah, I remember. What's wrong, Uncle" —I sneer—"too scared to face me yourself even in a projection?"

"Careful, Vivian. If you tease the bear, you might get the claws. I'm humoring you by not disconnecting, if you will, from the boy and shorting out his brain forever. The least you owe me is respect."

He's lying. I know it as surely as I know he's also prolonging this discourse for his own sick amusement. "Just tell me what I want before *I* end this."

He laughs loudly as though he's genuinely amused. "Oh, Vivian, I do miss your fire, your supreme though misguided arrogance! I thought you were like your parents, but the longer I know you, the more I think you and I are birds of a feather." He sighs tiredly. "I allowed Griffin to go to his mother's grave because he thought he could actually convince Wyck of his mistakes. It was no great surprise he would go there. I allowed it to show Griffin the error of his own naiveté. To think he actually believed he was that persuasive." He gives a mental head shake. "I do love his enthusiasm. His innocence, though, needs some adjustment. One would think having his twin, his own flesh, nearly beat him to death would rid him of it." He sighs again. "Oh well, we shall see. I ordered them not to take you all, of course. *I* will be the one to bring you back to your birthplace, to your home. Never doubt that."

"Yeah, I've heard that before, and I can definitely handle seeing my father, so out with it." Time to go. Easton's shaking beneath my hand, and a nauseous feeling creeps into my stomach when I realize I actually am hurting him.

Hoyt's essence begins to drift away from me. As his presence fades, he murmurs cryptically, "You already have it, my dear." As his voice drifts to nothing, he says, "Ah, 'to sleep perchance to dream'..."

CHAPTER EIGHTEEN

End Game

Her screams echo obscenely
throughout the facility.
He paces the narrow hallway,
angry at his
inability to reach her,
angry at me
for having delivered them
to this point.
Knowing she was carrying,
I gave her to them,
lead the charge,
disguised as him,
of course.
He returned to us after our success.
He could not hide
from me,
his only flesh and blood —
no, not his only,
not anymore.
They tried to run,
would have escaped,

but I could not allow that to happen.
She carries the ultimate weapon
in her womb.
She carries his power and hers.
Laying hands on her,
I saw inside their minds,
but felt only the power
of *the* one.
I know
without doubt
that we will finally have it.
For months, I have communed with them,
powers of the one
growing with each day,
while my brother
wept and begged,
pleading with her to forgive him,
trying to make her understand.
She must have read his heart
and his mind,
discerned the truth,
for she looks on me
with only disgust and
hatred.
But the ache inside me gratefully gave way
to emptiness
and a desire to
finally
have what we wanted, what the cause
needs.
He plots escape again, escape with them.
Still wants a life with a wife and children,
still believes that's possible.
He is a fool.

CHAPTER NINETEEN

"IT'S FROM *HAMLET*," Coop says with a mouth full of chips. We all stare at him like he's grown another head, but he only nods sagely. "Yep, in that part where he's talkin' about offin' himself."

"How do you know that?" Easton voices what we are all thinking.

"Mrs. Crafton made us watch it." He shrugs. " 'To sleep perchance to dream.' " He stuffs in another chip. Crumbs fall to the front of his orange shirt. "Yep, she made us write about what we thought he ought to do. I can't believe you don't remember that."

Easton raises one eyebrow. "Tutoring, dude." He drops his arm around my shoulder where we sit next to each other on the scratchy couch.

Cooper laughs. "Yeah, you probably didn't do it. Anyhow, that's what it's from." He looks around at the shocked faces in the living room area. Abby plops down on his lap and grabs a chip from the bag.

"I'm impressed, sweetie. You're, like, a closet genius or something," she says, smiling and crunching the edge of the chip.

Wyck stifles a yawn behind his hand. "A real Einstein. But we still don't know what Matthews meant by it. Is it something to do with the character of Hamlet or one of the other characters, or is it a reference to suicide? Could be your dad's hiding where the play's set, or maybe it's just his idea of a psycho joke?" He glances down at his watch. "I gotta go to bed, guys. It's almost 2:00 am. We can figure all this out in the morning."

"Yeah, as much as I hate to admit it, you're right. We'll all be clearer after some sleep. We can decipher it later," Easton says, yawning loudly.

Wyck goes into the bedroom and returns with a sheet, blanket, and pillow. "These were in the closet." He motions for Easton and me to stand. "You two are on my bed."

"Right," I say, feeling slightly guilty that the four of us will be hogging the beds yet again. As Cooper, Abby, and Easton shuffle sleepily into the bedroom, I turn to follow when I hear Wyck sigh loudly.

"Great," he mumbles.

When I turn back to him, he's taken off his shirt and is peering down at his abdomen where a three-inch scrape glares angrily from the flat muscles of his stomach, a bright red streak that's not deep but is probably uncomfortable.

I take the shirt that still dangles from his fingers in front of him. "What happened?" I ask just to have something to say since it obviously must have happened at the cemetery.

Eyes still not meeting mine, he gingerly touches it. "I didn't notice it earlier when I changed my shirt after we got here." In his distant voice and his downcast glance, he's reliving that encounter with his brother. I recall the blood splattered on his t-shirt after we escaped and Hoyt's words 'nearly beat him to death.'

"Guess I scraped something on Griff's belt."

I push him to the couch, and he doesn't resist. "I'm going to see if I can find a first-aid kit."

In the bathroom cabinet I find a dusty but fully-stocked first-aid kit.

"What are you doin'?" Easton mumbles groggily from the bed on my left.

"Wyck's got a cut. I'm just going to clean it." He only grumbles unintelligibly and rolls over.

Wyck is holding his head in his hands, elbows braced on his knees when I return. "Lie down." I sit on the floor beside the couch and take out a sealed alcohol pad, some antibiotic cream, and two wide Band-Aids.

"It's fine. You don't have to." He hisses in a breath through clenched teeth. "Ow, Princess! That burns!" He squirms, so I put my hand on his side.

"Oh, stop being a baby." I swipe the alcohol pad over his stomach again, but this time I blow on the cut until I realize he's no longer squirming away but is, instead, completely still. When I look up at him through my lashes, I realize he's holding his breath, and his eyes are an intense, dark blue. I sit up quickly, and he swallows audibly. I hand over the cream. "Here, spread this on."

"Yeah, that's probably for the best—for both of us," he says, disappointed but maybe a little relieved, too.

I open the Band-Aids, trying to forget yet another awkward moment, while Wyck smears on the antibiotic cream. I hand them to him to cover the scratch and gather my supplies to leave before I can further embarrass either one of us, but he touches my shoulder.

"Thanks, Princess," he says, dropping his eyes to my full hands.

"For what?" I ask, shaking my head.

"For that," he replies, nodding toward the Band-Aid wrappers and ointment. "For givin' a shit about me. You're the only person who's tried to take care of me in a long time." He smiles sadly, looking into a past I can't see. "Griffin used to do that." He meets my gaze again. "Try to doctor me." He shakes his head. "Seems like I was always getting hurt, and he was always picking up the pieces." He sighs. "Ironic thing to remember on a day when I…" He shakes his head. "Yeah, enough of that."

I stand, but he calls out. "Hey, you think maybe that dream earlier was a memory of Matthews?"

I shake my head. "The voice wasn't like a brother-to-brother kind of tone. It felt like he was talking to a child, like a parent-kid thing, you know? Besides, when was the last time you gave your brother a flower?"

"Oh, right. Guess I'm tired," he says with a yawn. He wrestles with the sheet and blanket and loses.

"Stand up," I command while setting down my supplies again. When he does, I spread out the sheet and arrange the pillow. "Now lie down."

His brows draw together. "I can cover up myself." He yawns widely again.

"Just do it." When he does, I fluff the blanket up and over him. "Sleep well, Wyck."

I turn to go, but he yanks me down by the hand, and his soft lips press against my cheek. Before I can react, he rolls over to face the back of the couch, away from me. But for the first time, I'm not worried about Easton's reaction or Wyck's intentions.

This is not a kiss, kiss. It's a thank you between friends, an 'I just want you to know how much I care' kiss.

"Sweet dreams, Princess," he mumbles sleepily, and I really hope he's right.

CHAPTER TWENTY

DAMN HOYT AND HIS CRYPTIC MESSAGES. For two days now I've played and replayed our conversation, hoping each time to have some epiphany complete with a cartoon light bulb over my head, but so far, I've got nothing. Well, nothing but a headache that is. We've overstayed our visit to what Abby has affectionately dubbed the love shack, but the rest has been good for all of them. Me, I'm going crazy here—no sleep, no location, and no clue what to do next. That's the real reason we haven't taken off yet. I'm supposed to be leading us, and I've got no idea where we need to go.

When we escaped the facility I thought I knew; I thought it would be easy. After all, even that smidgeon of Hoyt's memory seemed like a lot to go on, and I felt so close to my dad. In Hoyt's mind, he was right there, living and breathing, just waiting for me to fall down the rabbit hole and find him. I was naïve to think I could simply jump in a car and magically drive right to him. A little girl's dream.

"Hey, you comin' in, Vivian?" Cooper drawls as he walks past me, removing his t-shirt as he goes.

"Nah, I'm good." I fake a smile, like I'm not contemplating diving into that lake with a huge rock tied around my neck. Ugh! It's so frustrating, waiting for the answer to a question I don't know if I even need to ask. Apparently, I've already got the answer, whatever that means. The others have been great; no one has mentioned the fact that we're spinning our wheels here in the middle of nowhere until I figure it out. I think they're all pretending this is a real summer vacation with ordinary teenagers instead of a hiatus from crazyville.

Abby squeals when Cooper cannonballs from the tree limb sticking out over the water like a helping hand, where generations have taken the plunge. Wyck and Easton laugh when Cooper emerges right next to Abby and tosses her end-over-end, her legs and arms flailing as she sputters in mock anger.

"Come in, babe," Easton calls with a grin. "You've been lying on that blanket for hours."

I pull Abby's spare sunglasses off of my face and rub my eyes, which burn with fatigue. I haven't slept since I tapped into Hoyt through Easton's brain, and the wear is starting to weigh me down like an evil curse. "I think I need a nap. You guys enjoy yourselves. We'll have to get back on the road soon." Yeah, right, *if* I can figure out where we're going.

"Do it one last time before you go to sleep, V, please," Abby begs as she slicks back her wet hair and shakes water from her hands and arms.

"Sure." I smile, this time for real. Closing my eyes, I concentrate. At the sound of gushing water and Abby's laughter, I know I've succeeded without opening my eyes.

"That is so cool! My best friend can do, like, the most amazing trick ever!" Abby exclaims as the enormous fountain of shooting water I've created splashes back down into the rippling lake as if a geyser erupted. This has been a source of great amusement for her once we discovered I could shoot water into the air twenty feet just by willing it to do so. Truthfully, it's kind of cool, and it's been good practice for me. I think I might have this Water Element thing under control, at least when I'm fully awake. It's rained every night since we got here as I've tossed and turned, digging in my brain like a dog with a bone, and I have a feeling all the rain's been my fault.

Staring up through the living lace of the tree's leaves, I let my brain drift through images of blue prom orchids and weed-covered iron gates until the last few months swirl in a muted blur. Blissful sleep tugs my lids, and my drowsy brain struggles to remember Hoyt's words. What were they? Something about sleeping... dreaming...

* * *

Lines of different hues and sizes, numbers in tiny boxes. A map. A colorful map, brimming with the names of towns and forests. Roads crisscrossing in intricate, nonsensical disarray. A hand, slim male fingers, pointing to a circle drawn in black marker.

"Here," he says, an obvious smile in his voice even if his face is invisible. "This is where we're going next month. A whole week of sun and fun in the big city."

A female voice, "Show me where we are. You know I'm no good at these maps."

Rich laughter, a symphony of kept promises and reassuring hugs. "I'm going to need your help navigating, you know? Don't worry. I've traced it out." A slender finger points to a dark red line. "We are here, and we'll take highway…"

* * *

"Wake up, babe."

I open my eyes to vivid aqua eyes and a sexy grin. Water drips down Easton's cheek from the saturated ends of his hair, making the shaggy locks even darker than usual. He leans close and brushes his cool lips across my cheek.

"Time to get up, Sleeping Beauty."

"Does that make you my prince?" I murmur and pull him close so that his wet torso and arms press against my borrowed pink bikini.

He chuckles. "I somehow doubt you need rescuing, but I'll be your prince if it makes you smile like this." He touches my face. "I was afraid you'd forgotten how. Don't think I've seen one since we got here."

I realize he's right. I haven't had much cause to smile, and I'm not entirely sure what's brought it on now, but I feel completely elated, beyond happy.

He cocks his head to the side and lifts one brow. "I wish I was the cause of all this happiness, but I don't think I am. Something's happened. What is it, babe?" he asks, his gaze reminding me of one of Wyck's probing looks.

I shrug. He's right. This joy is coming from something besides the teenage dream pressing against me, but I feel too good to over-analyze at the moment, complete relief. "I took a nap. Must be that." I shrug, not wanting to think too hard about it. Looking around, I notice we're alone. "Where is everyone else?"

"Headed back to the cabin for some food," he says. "Buuuuuttttt" — he wiggles his eyebrows as he drags out the word — "we could hang out here awhile, just the two of us, if you want."

I giggle and squeeze his broad shoulders. "Oh yeah? And do what, Easton?" I kiss his earlobe, and he shudders slightly.

"I don't know." He skims his hand along my hip and side before dipping his lips to the rapidly-increasing pulse in my throat. "A little fun in the sun?"

Fun in the sun. The statement from my dream jars through my head like a ringing bell, and I jump up, knocking Easton to the side. "That's it! That's why I'm so happy!"

Sitting up on his elbows, his expression is more than a little annoyed as he gawks at me. "Babe, you're supposed to be happy *after* we make out."

"No!" I laugh and grab both his cheeks, squishing his face together. "My dream! Fun in the sun! When you said that, it brought back my dream!" I kiss his smooshed lips and release his cheeks. "The map! I saw the map! I know where we're going!"

CHAPTER TWENTY-ONE

"HERE!" I POINT TO A SPOT on the map we found buried in a stack of old magazine. "This is where the circle was in my dream!"

"Are you sure, Princess?" Wyck asks from his position beside me, his head tilted and his brows drawing together. "There doesn't seem to be anything there."

"Yeah, V, there's, like, not a town or anything." Abby hops up on the corner of the table where we've spread the map and wrinkles the far corner of it.

"Ab!" I yank it from beneath her hip. "Yes, I'm sure. In my dream, this"—I jab again at the area—"was circled."

"But how do you know it wasn't just a regular dream? Why do you think it's your dad?" Cooper grabs a soda from the fridge.

I glance at Wyck, but he only raises his brows as though he thinks Cooper might have a valid question. Thanks a lot, buddy.

"Yes, I think it was." At the expressions on all of their faces, I shake my head. "It makes sense, Hoyt's mysterious quote about sleeping and dreaming. I think he was giving me a message, a way I could see my father."

"But we still don't know if these are his old memories or what," Wyck says, shrugging. "Is this where he is or was? Is this now or sometime in his past, maybe even a memory with your mom? You said you heard a woman. He could have planted that in your head somehow."

I sigh in exasperation. "No, I didn't say it was a woman. I said it was a female."

"What's the difference?" Wyck throws up his hands in frustration.

"There's a difference, okay?" I glare at him. No one seems impressed with the importance of my dream or this location. "Yeah, he could have planted it, but I've been thinking about that. How would it be a memory with my mom? Hoyt would never have seen them planning a getaway. I don't think she knew about him until"—I pause as my stomach lurches thinking about how terrifying my mother must have been when the Liaisons came for her—for us—"until they took her away to the facility. This... memory or vision or whatever wasn't a frightening one. They weren't panicked or anything like that. They were planning a vacation. Hoyt would never have seen that." I shake my head again. "No, this wasn't a trick. It was too real."

"Then it couldn't be now if there was a woman in the dream." Easton walks away from us and plops down on the couch. I stare at him quizzically. "It couldn't be now if it was your mom, right?"

"So maybe your dad has a new family?" Abby's feet dangle from her perch on the table.

All the air rushes from my lungs and I feel as though I've been gut-punched. Easton gasps, Wyck rubs his face, and Cooper open-mouth stares at her.

"What?" she innocently asks. "He could have! It's been a long time since he was with... since he left... crap! You know what I mean! He could have started another family by now." She crosses her arms like a child, her brows drawing down over her eyes, and grumbles, "I didn't mean it to hurt your feelings, V. I was just stating the obvious."

And I know what she means. In fact, I can't believe I didn't put two and two together myself. That has to be it, but I just didn't want to see the truth in it. He's moved on. My life has gone to hell in a hand basket, and he's moved on. He probably has a two-story, three-bath on Happy Lane, USA, and I'm homeless!

Anger suddenly overwhelms warm and fuzzy, and my motivation shifts into revenge. I'm going to find him now if for no other reason than to wreak havoc on his pristine life.

When my stomach retreats from my throat, I walk over to Abby and wrap my arms around her. "It's okay, Ab. You're absolutely right. I'm glad you had the good sense to say it." Her tense shoulders relax when she returns my embrace.

"We'll find him, *and* his new family. And then we'll beat the crap out of them."

I laugh. "You read my mind, friend."

CHAPTER TWENTY-TWO

Goodbye

"Thank you, brother."
Snow as soft as down
covers his hair,
catches in his lashes.
"Don't thank me yet."
He grabs my hand,
like he did when we
were boys,
hiding during a storm.
"Don't do this.
Don't you have a shred
of humanity left inside
that husk
that used to be my
brother?"
"I just used it."
I cannot tell him
of my sadness,
my regret
at having to hurt him.
Turning, I catch a glimpse.

A bundle in the backseat.
"You aren't taking much.
What a shame
this is what you've chosen!"
"I didn't have a choice, remember?"
Fury radiates
in the clench of fists
at his sides,
in the tightened jaw,
in the heaviness of the snowfall.
"No, brother,
I'm the one with no choice.
You were determined to flee,
regardless of my warnings.
They would come for you,
and I refuse to see
you die for *this*.
I have told you,
I will always choose
your life
over hers."
"Over theirs."
"No, hers.
I will have it,
with
or without
the mother."
He yanks me into an embrace
shoulders shaking,
silently begging,
begging me for their lives.
If I still had a heart,
it would be breaking.
"Why not let me take both of them?
You could arrange it.
Fake their deaths, too."
He will never understand.

He is,
has always been,
my only priority.
I close my eyes,
pull away from him.
Regretful
over what can never be.
"I will triumph,
reclaim my genetic masterpiece.
I will use it as it was always intended."
My supreme victory.
"She! She, not it!
And she is only a child!
Bring her to me!
Stop this madness, brother!"
"Go, before I change my mind."
"Promise me,
if you find my child,
you will not hurt her."
I turn from the torture of those eyes,
his eyes,
never mine again.

CHAPTER TWENTY-THREE

AFTER PLANNING OUR NEWEST ADVENTURE, we spent one more night in the cabin and headed out the next morning. I insisted Easton and Cooper call home and Abby leave a message for her parents to explain that we had found my father, which is only a tiny lie on the great lie meter of life. We did find him, sort of. At this point I figure my lie meter has skyrocketed past the red and is now spinning wildly out of control. What's one more?

We've been on the road for days—again! That's been the theme of this summer. I'm so sick of traveling that if I never go anywhere again, it'll be too soon. But our journey is almost over, I think.

"This is the road, babe," Easton says from behind the wheel. His raised brows tell me he's awaiting my permission to make what we all hope is the final turn. He holds up the map, which has been folded and refolded until the creases have created roads of their own. "This is the circled road."

I shake my head and swallow hard, having lost most of my bravado somewhere along the way. Abby leans between the front seats and squeezes my shoulder.

"Whatever we find, we'll deal with it, V." I smile sickly, put my hand over hers, and wonder when Abby become the strong one.

I nod my head. "Let's do it, Easton." He returns my nod as we pull down the gravel road that's little more than a mountain path. The deep ruts slow us to a snail's pace and give me plenty of time to work myself up. What if he isn't here anymore? What if he is?

What if he rejects me immediately or tells me he never cared about my mother? My stomach rolls like I'm riding some rapids in a holey kayak.

A million bumps, three chewed fingernails, and a low-water bridge later, we round a leafy bend. To our right is a large house with a veranda-style, wraparound porch. The wood planking covering the outside and the rough-hewn, wooden posts and railings create the illusion that the surrounding forest might have actually created the house. Vibrant orange and red flowers line the porch, and a birdhouse swings from a straw rope on the corner of the porch. The entire scene oozes peace and tranquility. Too bad I've forgotten what those emotions feel like right now.

Easton reaches over and gently tugs my hand down from my mouth but not before I've managed to mangle another nail.

"Do you want me to pull in the drive?" he asks, his blue-green gaze as anxious as my own.

Speech has abandoned me, so I just nod. He turns the SUV onto the multi-hued paving stones of the drive. When we pass the mailbox, all of us turn to stare at the 'Matthews' painted in cheery yellow paint on the over-sized box. It's a perfect complement to the Brown-Eyed Susans and Queen Anne's Lace growing nearly as tall as the post on which the box rests.

"Think we found it," Coop drawls right before Abby whacks him on the arm.

When Easton pulls to a stop and cuts the ignition, no one moves.

"What do you want to do now?" Easton asks. I can feel all of their eyes on me, waiting for a meltdown or an explosion of some sort. But now that I'm actually facing my destiny, I have no idea what to do.

Quick as a flash, my door opens and Wyck is standing beside me. "We'll find out together," he says, echoing my own words as we approached the cemetery looking for his mother.

He takes my hand as I step out of the vehicle, and I grip his hand so tightly I know I have to be hurting him. Thunder booms overhead, and clouds begin to congregate above us.

Wyck glances up. "This you? You're gonna have to work on this, you know?" He smiles kindly as I hear doors slamming. The others follow suit and step up behind us. When we're about to step onto the natural-stone steps of the porch, I panic.

"Wait!" My breath saws rapidly in and out of my chest, and my hand is shaking so badly that when I reach for a porch post to steady myself, I miss it entirely on the first attempt.

"This is what I want, right?" I ask no one in particular. I search the eight pairs of eyes. Raindrops make dark circles on the shoulders of their t-shirts. "I have to do this, right? Right?!"

Wyck moves his face directly in my line of sight. "You *need* to do this." He shakes his head and steps up onto the porch. As he drags me across to the screen door, all I can do is shake my head. He's right. I have to know. I have to see him, confront him, ask him about my mother, and my background.

He opens the screen door and knocks. We wait. And wait. And wait. He knocks again then tries the doorknob. It twists easily. After glancing over at me, he opens it and we walk inside.

I'm immediately surprised by the organized chaos of the room. The overstuffed chairs and the worn couch don't even come close to matching. Lamps of various sizes and shapes stand sentry on end tables of unfinished wood. Dried wildflowers and roses hang in bundles near a doorway across the room. The walls are rough wood planks only slightly smoother than those lining the outside of the house. A worn staircase to the right leads up to a second story. The huge, dark green rope rug and oddball picture frames (that I don't want to examine too closely at the moment) remind me of the home I shared with Aunt Charlotte, and the whole place smells like a rich cherry tobacco, sweet but rugged at the same time. It's all so clean and cozy. This is a home—a real, honest-to-goodness home—and my jealousy overwhelms me.

The rain pounds the roof and slips in rivulets down the window panes, obscuring the tree line into a green blur. From somewhere in the back of the house, a door slams, and musical, female laughter jars me from my inspection.

"Where'd that rain come from?" Familiar female laughter moves toward the doorway directly across from me, and I know in a matter of seconds I'll meet my dream in the flesh. "I'm going to grab a blanket for Petey then I'll make us some coff—"

Our gasps are as identical as our gray eyes.

CHAPTER TWENTY-FOUR

I'M MESMERIZED, and judging by her steady gaze, I'd say she is, too. Our features are so similar that it's clear we're related. Same height (or rather lack thereof), same weight, same nose, but the eyes are the clincher, as gray as the storm clouds weeping overhead. The only significant difference is our hair. Where mine is a reddish-brown, hers is as golden as a wheat field. Even through the dampness it's obvious the long tresses will dry a warm yellow, and the ends curl in nearly-perfect ringlets on the shoulders of her pink button-down. This is my sister, the girl from my dream. We look so much alike, but that can mean only one thing.

We stand unblinking, my brain refusing to completely process what the reality must be and the rain beating time with my heart, until an enormous, chocolate-brown Labrador Retriever skids to a stop at her feet. All paws and slobber, the dog barks loudly and slaps her blue jeans with his wagging tail. He shakes his wide body and showers her with water droplets.

"Petey! Stop!" she yells, the spell broken.

"Honey, what's taking so—," a man calls cheerily as he approaches from behind. This is him. This is the man from my dreams. My father.

My first thought is how much he resembles Hoyt, tall and attractive, but with lighter hair, more blond than brown. My second thought is how beautiful his eyes are, brilliant moss green, as shocking as stumbling from the desert into a medieval forest. I know instinctually that these eyes are what mother loved most about his features. They must have drawn her like a doomed moth to a flame, lured her as surely as he could beguile me into trusting him if I allow it.

"Violet?" His voice breaks, shatters into a thousand tiny fragments. He raises his fist to his mouth as though he's trying to hold back the emotion struggling for release.

"What's going on, Dad?" the girl beside him asks, turning her face to his like a sunflower to the morning sky.

That one-syllable word, which has guided my path and shaped more than the events of the last few months, is my undoing.

I'm vaguely aware that Wyck's hand rests in mine, and I pause only briefly to take in the shocked expressions on the faces of my band of misfits. They've formed a physical barrier at my back as though they're protecting me from my past but not this future standing three steps in front of me. I yank my hand roughly from Wyck's. His stunned, indigo eyes nearly keep me rooted to the spot—but not quite.

I barrel past my friends and let the screen door slam behind me as I bound off the porch. My Converses slip on the wet grass. The rain sheets around me, and I'm drenched in a matter of seconds.

"Vivian! Wait!" Easton stands at the open door, moving toward me, but I want to be alone. I don't know what I'm feeling, and I don't have the emotional armor for a conversation right now.

I sprint toward the woods surrounding the house and run until my legs carry me where my heart knew I needed to go all along. The lake from my dream looms before me, rippling madly as the rain pounds into it. The image of the purple flower and the feeling of love and safety—those were hers, his other daughter's, not mine. I let myself hope for a home, and for that, I deserve to be hurt.

In my mind I've alternated between loving and hating this man since I was old enough to realize what I was missing, but the reality is he wasn't mine to do either. *She* is his daughter... my twin, and he chose her over me. He kept her locked away here, isolated and safe, and left my mother and me to run. In a weird way, he has betrayed me, my mother's memory, and Aunt Charlotte's myriad sacrifices. No matter what happens, I'm not sure there is enough forgiveness inside of what's left of my heart.

Thunder rumbles around me and the hard-pounding rain stings my bare arms and face. Lightning forks down across the lake with a deafening boom while my body begins to tingle. The tiny hairs on the back of my neck stand up. When my hand glows bright blue, I know what's coming next. I will it to happen. I need this, have needed it for so long. It's a connection to my mother and our last moments together.

Lightning strikes again, this time much closer, and though I know my Gift will protect me, I still jump at the sound and force. While the storm's fury swirls around me, I close my eyes and beg it to take away my own fury. I extend my arms, palms up. When the lightning explodes, an orb forms above my hands. My vision tunnels gray-white then starbursts.

I open my eyes to an azure world of energy waves pulsating from the Earth itself, and for the first time in weeks, I'm at peace. The storm is leeching my anger at my non-father, my frustration at never having a normal family, my jealousy at this girl I don't even know who's innocent in all of this, and my complete astonishment that I never knew about my twin.

"Vivian!" Easton calls from behind me.

I turn to see him burst through the trees lining the lake. His t-shirt has formed a second skin, hugging his tight chest and stomach while water runs down the planes of his face, making his eyes more vivid. Even with his hair plastered to his head, my heart leaps at the sight of him.

"Easton, stay back!" I yell as the lightning leaps into my open hands once again.

The storm may be the work of my subconscious, but now that it's in full effect I'm not entirely sure how to stop it. But with Easton's arrival, the calm blossoming inside of me spreads quickly, and the rain's force diminishes along with the thunder and lightning.

Easton doesn't wait for me to call him over. Shaking the water from his head and body like the Lab from minutes ago, he walks toward me and pulls me to him. For what feels like an eternity, neither of us speak, and I'm breathing easier when he finally releases me.

"How'd you find me?" I ask, gazing up into his eyes.

He chuckles. "Are you kidding me? How do I always find you?"

Smiling, I rest my head against his chest. "Good point," I murmur.

"Besides, I've sort of already lived this scene once before, remember?"

For a second I don't know what he's talking about, then I remember the lake back home and the night he witnessed my freakishness in living color.

"Yeah, I guess you did." I can't hide the strain in my voice, don't really try. All of this is just another reminder of how screwed up my entire existence is.

Stepping away from me, he holds me at arm's length as though he's afraid I'll bolt if given the chance. Sprinkles of rain plop between us.

"So, you ready to face this instead of running away like a coward?"

I cringe. He's absolutely right, but that doesn't make hearing it said aloud any easier. I've wanted this for so long, and now that we're here, I can't NOT do it. Twin or no twin, this is my father, and I've faced worse. Taking a deep breath, I grasp Easton's wrists and pull his hands from my upper arms.

"I hope so." I try to fortify myself with a smile, but it twists into a grimace.

He shakes his head and gifts me with his lopsided grin. "You can face down a homicidal madman with crazy-strong powers, but one girl, who looks uncannily like you by the way, sends you running for cover?"

"I'm not good with normal." I manage a real smile this time when he tilts his head and quirks one brow. "Okay, normal and I are about the same distance away as the moon. Semi-normal then?"

He smiles, mega-watt this time, then grows serious. "Whatever happens, *we* will face it, you, me, Abby, Cooper, and Wyck. We're all in this with you. We can handle anything, normal or abnormal. You've seen your dad!" He smiles again and squeezes my hands. "Sure, it was only for like thirty seconds, but still! You've done it! You've made your wish come true!"

And even though I smile with my lips, it doesn't quite reach my soul. What's that old saying? Be careful what you wish for; you just might get it. Yeah, then you get dragged back to face it in your sopping clothes. Not ideal.

CHAPTER TWENTY-FIVE

THE SMELL OF COFFEE WAFTS from the screen door, and I take a deep breath as we slog up the stone steps, slick with the still-falling rain. It would all seem so welcoming if not for the uncanny quiet inside. Only the occasional sound of throat clearing emerges.

When I hesitate again, Easton huffs a breath and yanks my hand, forcing me to either climb the steps or fall on my face, which I'm seriously considering as the better option, until I hear Abby. She's going for light and friendly but sounds like her panties are cutting off the oxygen to her brain.

"So, Mr. Matthews, I'm sure this is all, like, completely shocking to you and... um... your daughter, but Vivian's really excited to see you—that is she will be... when she comes back."

Then a loudly muttering Coop, "You mean *if* she comes back."

"Cooper! Oh course she'll come back!" That a girl, Abby! She sounds confident, but I'll bet she's just as unsure of that outcome as Cooper is.

Guess they've introduced themselves. I didn't really leave them many options, though. Easton holds open the door then ushers me, dripping and anxious. I say a little prayer that my stomach doesn't choose this moment to rebel. That would not make this situation any better. When all heads swing my way, I'm pretty sure it might happen.

Abby jumps up from her spot on the tired couch and rushes over, stopping when she realizes I'm soaked. Her relief at my appearance is touching until she gives me a death glare worthy of my old principal.

"V! Where have you been?" she asks in a strained, saccharine voice. "I was just assuring Mr. Matthews you'd be right back." Her eyelids are pulled back so far that the whites are visible all around the blue of her eyes, magnified by her purple-framed glasses. I shiver slightly, and she turns to the man who is my father. "Mr. Matthews, could we get a towel for Vivian?"

For the first time since reentering the room, I peer over at him where he's standing beside the doorway, leaning in shock against the doorway. When our eyes meet, he straightens stiffly and takes a step toward me. He has the same shocked expression he did when I ran out, green eyes staring with an unnerving intensity, like he's trying to decide if I'm real or the monster in some horrendous nightmare.

"Mr. Matthews?" Abby repeats.

He jumps a little and shakes his head. "Of course!" He turns to *the girl*, my would-be sister I suppose. "Honey, please get her a towel." Nodding, she rises quickly from the recliner, rushing through the doorway beside him. To her retreating form, he calls out, "Bring two, Charlotte."

The name is a gunshot to my chest. Abby and I gasp in unison. I whip my eyes back to him.

"Charlotte?" I squeak out through my tight throat. I try to take a deep breath, but my lungs have forgotten their purpose. "Her, her name is Charlotte?"

I don't hear his reply since my knees have chosen that moment to buckle, and I latch onto Abby. "I think I need to sit down," I whisper, my voice hoarse with emotion.

Easton's hand grasps my arm as he guides me to the spot Abby vacated on the couch. Cooper and Wyck appear in front of me, and I don't need to see all of their faces to know the same disbelief I'm feeling is mirrored in their eyes. The girl—Charlotte—must have returned because Abby kneels beside me with a fluffy, white towel. She gathers the oversized terrycloth in her hands and begins to swipe it gently over my face and arms. Maybe it's her concern, maybe it's the silent support battalion of teenagers surrounding me, or maybe it's seeing my long lost father and his new family—hell, it's probably all three—but I am overwhelmed with emotions. When the tears start, Abby wipes them, too.

"Thanks." Easton mumbles. Then he too begins to wipe down his arms.

A huge snout noses between Wyck and the couch, right into my face. Eyes of creamy hazel seem to radiate concern as the Lab whimpers softly. He nudges into my side, leaving me covered in the smell of wet dog, but his big, warm body comforts me somehow, and I tentatively brush a hand over his back. I've never considered myself an animal person, but we bond immediately, leaving me wondering if it's because of the girl who has rocked my entire existence. Do twins have the same scent? I want to laugh hysterically at my completely inappropriate thought. It's official. I'm losing it.

"Petey, leave her alone." Charlotte's lyrical voice drifts through the forest of legs and my fogged brain.

"He's fine." I stroke his damp fur.

Abby ruffles my hair with the towel before wrapping it around my shoulders. "Thanks, Ab."

She smiles sympathetically at me and whispers, "We'll get through this together." Again, I'm struck by how truly fortunate I am to have this support group. As screwed up as this whole situation is, I don't think I'd survive it without them.

"So, what happens now?" I ask no one in particular. When I get no response, I take Petey's big head in my hands. "Any ideas, Petey?" His head-tilted, puzzled expression says it all. "I feel the same way, boy." Petey barks loudly and hops excitedly with his front paws.

Wiping my face, I sigh then stand. The sea of bodies parts. Easton nods his head in support, and clasping the towel closed in front of me like a shield, I walk determinedly toward father.

CHAPTER TWENTY-SIX

HOW DO YOU GREET A GUY who abandoned you and your mother to save his own butt while apparently choosing to care for your sister? Just as I'm trying to decide whether to stick out my hand for a formal intro, he crosses the remaining distance and yanks me to him in a bone-crusher hug. Stiff as a mannequin, I tense until I realize his shoulders are shaking and he's crying on my shoulder.

Crap! I want to hate him, but I can feel my heart shifting, melting. This man—my dad—regrets. I know it as certainly as I knew Petey was offering his doggy comfort less than a minute ago, so I do what I normally would never do and tap into his mind, treading softly rather than a full-on assault.

I have her back. She's come back to me after all these years. She looks so much like Violet it almost hurts to look at her.

Crap, crap, crap! The ice in my chest cracks. I don't want to like him, dammit! But how can I not when he is so obviously relieved, happy even, to see me? Then I sense a shift in his mood.

Oh no! She's here! If she's here, he'll be here soon! How will I protect them?

He must mean Hoyt. He's freaking inside when he pulls back from me, and the panic is evident in the tense lines around his eyes and lining his forehead. His concern for me takes me back. He does care about me, so much so that his first thoughts are fear for my safety. But that doesn't make his leaving my mom and me any better.

Regardless of his reasons for leaving my mother and me all those years ago and his reasons for seducing her in the first place, he cares for me. The fissure in my frigid heart becomes a little wider with the hope that I could have a family again, a father who looks at me the same way he looks at my sister, with the same love in his voice when he spoke to her in my dreams.

With his fear comes the realization I'm in his mind. After a minute of surprise, he tilts his head, looking like the dog. He smiles knowingly.

"Why am I not surprised? Your mother used to do the same thing," he says tenderly, sadly, but the smile vanishes quickly. "We have to leave. I won't let you go again."

"No, we have a lot to talk about... everything," I smile tentatively. His smile widens, and he yanks me to him again, shattering the ice wide open.

*   *   *

"And now we're here." Sighing, I finish off my cup of coffee and draw the blanket tighter around my shoulders, shivering but not from the temperature. For the past three hours and with some help from Easton, I've relived my seventeen years at Harrison's kitchen table. His first questions had been about my mother. When I told him that she had sacrificed herself to save me, he'd turned away and gripped the counter till his knuckles turned white. He'd stood that way, statuesque, for so long that I'd continued, filling in with broad strokes the details of my life with Aunt Charlotte until my fight in the cafeteria with Betty the She-man.

The last few months, I described in detail. I told my father everything—from the prom debacle to my dreams of him. Through it all he's said little and has only stopped me to ask the occasional question. But at least he's no longer attached to the counter. Instead, he's pacing.

I lean into Easton's side where we sit on the cushioned bench behind a scarred but charming cedar table. The quaint room reminds me of my Aunt Charlotte's kitchen where we spent so much time talking about everything. Easton drops his arm around my shoulder and caresses my arm. Harrison, pacing along the wall near the stove and cabinets, nods.

The others are sacked out in the living room despite the television blasting canned sitcom laughter. But not Charlotte. She has been sitting across from me for the entire, tedious explanation, glancing my way only when she thinks I'm not noticing. Whenever we make eye contact, she drops her gaze and picks at a chip in her coffee mug. I want so badly to read her mind, but the story has absorbed my attention, making it impossible to slip inside and explore.

A little piece of me, okay more like all of me, is hoping she's the bad twin. But I have this sneaking suspicion that thoughts like that are exactly why I'm not the good twin. She looks as though she's never even said a curse word before, and she seems to be taking all this very well. After the initial shock from our face-to-face in the living room, she's watched me with curiosity from beneath lowered lashes, leading me to think that maybe I'm the only sibling in the dark. Judging by her calm, she had to have known about me. And when I mentioned Aunt Charlotte, she had nodded knowingly, so he must have told her about her namesake, too. Figures. Everyone seems to know my life better than I do.

I keep reminding myself I'm not supposed to care, that I'm not here for my father's approval or to gain the support of a sister, but every time he stops pacing long enough to cast a sympathetic glance at me, it's like breadcrumbs from the master's table. I can't help myself; I'm steadily losing my battle with apathy, which just irritates the hell out of me. I really, really don't want to like him.

"Could you please stop pacing?" I bark. "You're making me more nervous than I already am."

From the doorway comes a snort of disbelief. "*You* are telling someone to stop pacing? The queen of pacing?" Wyck shakes his head and grins. "Sorry," he says, bowing at the waist, "the Princess of pacing."

I narrow my eyes as he snorts again. "I do not pace." He laughs and reaches for my coffee mug. "I don't!"

He turns up the mug to take a swig of the strong brew and frowns when he sees it's empty. "Princess, I'm surprised you haven't worn a hole in your shoes."

I nervously run my hand through my wet hair. He's completely right. Millions of people pace, right? Doesn't make me like my father because we share one nervous gesture, right?

Charlotte giggles. "Father does that, too."

"What?" I ask, again snagging my fingers through the snarl of my hair.

"That." She points at Harrison where he's leaning against the sink counter, running his hand through his own blondish locks.

We both stop, hands in hair. He shrugs in guilty confirmation. I immediately drop my hand.

Wyck plops onto the bench next to me, briefly squeezing my arm in silent support despite his joking manner. Easton's arm tightens just enough for me to know that he's still not 100 percent happy with my and Wyck's closeness, but the fact that Easton no longer feels the need to strangle Wyck shows how far he's come.

Taking a deep breath, I lock eyes with my father. "Your turn," I say a little more gruffly than I probably should. I can practically see the scowl on Aunt Charlotte's face. She would be less than pleased at my rudeness even to the father I'm not sure I can trust.

"Where would you like for me to start?" He waves around his open hand.

I cut my eyes to Charlotte and raise my brows in an are-you-kidding expression. "I think *she* would be a good starting point, don't you?" Charlotte's eyes widen.

"Well, Charlotte is your sister." Thank you Captain Obvious.

"Yeah, I guessed as much." I probably should at least try to keep the sarcasm out of my voice, but I can't. Aunt Charlotte would tell me to stop acting like a child, but right now the very thought of her name makes me even more angry. "We're twins, aren't we?"

"Yes, Vivian, you are." His brow crinkles in confusion. "You mean your mother never told you?" When I only continue glaring at him, he runs his hand through his disheveled hair again. "I suppose she didn't really get the chance, did she? At five years old, you wouldn't have really understood the... situation anyway." He drops his gaze as a palpable sadness consumes him. This man loved my mother; regardless of what happened or didn't happen, he loved, that soul-deep love that I have for Easton.

"I wish you both had known her. I had hoped to see her again someday." When he swipes at his cheek, my throat tightens. Charlotte rises and rubs his back as though she could wipe out his pain with that gesture. Her eyes remain dry as tears flood mine. But *she* never knew Violet; *I* did. The irrationality of staking a claim on our dead mother doesn't escape me, but I don't care enough to douse my possessiveness.

He raises his teary eyes as he reaches for her hand. I have to take a calming breath to keep from launching myself at the pair of them. They comfort each other. Who's been there to comfort me? What gives her the right to comfort him about a woman she didn't even know? I lost a mother! I lost the only parent I had, then I lost the woman who raised me, and now I have to watch these two? And he's no better! Mourning a woman—a life—he abandoned when he turned tail and ran like a coward! Irrational anger threatens to explode from my chest.

Sensing my rising emotion in my tense body, the boys on either side of me tense as well. This rollercoaster of feeling is leaving me nauseous. Not even Easton's hand tightening on my shoulder is going to make me feel better at the moment. He leans over so that we are eye-to-eye. Removing his arm from around my shoulders, he tugs my glowing hand to his chest.

"You need to calm down, babe," he whispers, trying to hide the obvious sign of my anger.

"Calm down? I should calm down?" My voice shakes, and when his face becomes illuminated by a soft white light, I know I'm too close to the edge. Answers or not, I need to get out of here, but I'm trapped between Easton and Wyck.

"Let me out." I turn toward Wyck who's blocking my way to the living room and front door. I push against his shoulder.

"Princess, you need to talk to—"

I stop him by holding up my blue palm. "Don't tell me what I need, Wyck. Now, move!"

"No," he calmly replies despite the murderous look I shoot him. He shifts his hips around effectively blocking any possible escape route. When I shift toward Easton, he cocks his head and lifts one eyebrow. Okay, clearly I'm getting no help from that side, and since I could never hurt Easton, I whip back to Wyck. By this time my father and sister are watching me intently. I can feel their eyes on me.

"Move your ass off this bench, Wyck," I grit out between clinched teeth, my breath coming rapidly.

"No," he says shaking his head, "you're gonna have to make me."

"Don't think I won't." I'm near panic. If I don't get out of this room and away from my newfound family soon, I'm going to combust.

"They're your family, Princess. You have to stop running and face them."

Suddenly, my brain goes into neutral, and my panic takes over. I lash out at the nearest target. "Like you faced your brother? Should I beat the hell out of them both?"

He blanches, his face draining of color, and Easton sucks in a breath behind me. I know I've gone too far when remorse screams inside my head, but I'm all 'flight or fight' mode, escape at any means.

Wyck drops his head and breathes deeply. I think I'm about to win this one, but when he lifts his head again, his eyes burn.

"I'm not moving, Vivian, no matter how nasty and hateful you're being," he says tightly. "You'll have to move me."

Nostrils flaring, chest heaving, I close my eyes. I'm afraid if I use my hand against him that I'll seriously hurt him, so I concentrate on my other weapon. When I hear a rumble in the wall behind the sink, I smirk. Harrison and Charlotte step away from the sink, staring down at it like they've never seen it before.

"I did warn you, Wyck, and don't forget that you're the one who told me to work on it."

The rumbling increases in volume and intensity right before water explodes from the knobs, propelling them across the room where they lodge in the wall behind Wyck's head. A flash of realization widens his eyes right before the gushing fountains angle toward Wyck, blasting him in the chest and face and sending him scurrying from the bench and onto the floor. Watching him sputter would be quite entertaining if I weren't so pissed off.

I climb over his legs and take off, past a still-sleeping Abby and Cooper, past a barking Petey, and past the picture frames of a family I don't know, doing things I've never done. I'm getting good at running. Too bad it never takes me anywhere.

CHAPTER TWENTY-SEVEN

Awe

Nearly five years of running,
of chasing,
but I have her.
She is so much stronger
with the child.
She feeds from her.
I wonder if
he
strengthens from the
other.
Tonight
I will kill her
and take the girl.
She will leave me no choice.
I've seen the depth of her love
for the girl.
and she will never
never
give her up willingly.
So
I will take her.

Being so close to the girl
overwhelms me.
I feel her power.
I feel her father
through her.
But the core of her,
that is her mother.
No matter.
I will take her back,
back
to the facility.
I will take her back,
back
to the cause.
Then I will bring home
the other one
and
my brother.

CHAPTER TWENTY-EIGHT

COOL AIR BATHES MY FACE as I burst from the doorway and onto the porch. Grabbing the porch post, I sink to the steps, still wet from the earlier rain. My anger vanishes faster than my jeans soak up the water. I suck in great gulps of the fresh air. Distance and the night make for a very sobering effect.

Shit! What have I done? I said such horrible things to Wyck right before blasting him with a kitchen-sink geyser! I wouldn't blame him if he never speaks to me again. And all because my sister comforted her father! No, it's more than that. It's... it's... everything! The trip, the worry, the frustration, and most importantly, the jealousy. I'm so jealous of Charlotte's life, her relationship with our father that I can hardly breathe. When I start to hyperventilate, I drop my head between my knees, my hands rammed into my tangled hair.

I don't realize I'm crying until I hear shuffled steps behind me and feel someone's hand on my shoulder. I'm about to shake it off when the someone sits down beside me and pulls me into an embrace. The rich smell of cherry tobacco clings to his shirt. I try to pull away, but he holds on tight, and I blubber openly on my father's shirt, gripping the front with both hands until I'm sure the fabric will never be the same again. He rubs my head, and it just feels so right that I cry harder. Only when I'm left with the post-sob hiccups bouncing my chest does he loosen his hold and allow me to pull back. I sit, head down, not daring to make eye contact.

"Well, you certainly screwed that up," he says lightly.

My head jerks up in open-mouth surprise only to find him smiling, his eyes twinkling in the moonlight. I nod but can't join in his good humor. "Yeah, guess so. That's me, queen of pacing and screwing up."

"That your first sink?" he asks, quirking his head.

"Yep, first kitchen I've ever assaulted. I'm really sorry," I say sheepishly, more than a little embarrassed at my childish behavior.

"Aw" — he waves his hand dismissively — "don't worry about that. I destroyed more than one in my day before I learned to control it. Besides, Charlotte's a tinker. She loves working around the house. It'll give her something to do and probably an excuse to repaint the kitchen, with you as her slave labor, of course." He smiles and rubs my knee before his expression becomes serious. "It's okay, Vivian. I'm not the one you need to apologize to." He raises his brows.

"I know." I nod again. "Why did I do that?!" I cover my face with my hands and mumble, "I'm such an asshole sometimes. I honestly don't know how or more importantly *why* they've put up with me all this time. I would have dumped me on the side of the road two hundred miles ago or, better yet, never have come looking for me in the first place. They should've run the other way when they found me in Mr. Lewis's diner."

He chuckles and forces my hands down. "I'm really glad they did, sweetheart. And I'm glad my brother chose Lewis as his Magnet."

"Why? I told you how badly he hurt Mr. Lewis. Why would you be glad he chose him?"

"Because Lewis would never have let him hurt you under his watch. He's a good man. I've known him a long time." He sighs and nods slowly.

"He told me." I hesitate, but I've come this far *and* destroyed his kitchen *and* hurt one of my dearest friends in the process, so what the hell. I go for it, dreading but needing the answer.

"He said he wasn't sure how you felt about my mother, but he thought you must have loved her by the way you looked at her. That true?" Like hair on a cat's back, my defenses go up as I watch him. If he says there was never anything real between them, the sink will be the least of his worries. I'm really not sure my bruised psyche can take anymore tonight without overloading.

Briefly, he looks away into the night sky, but when he turns back to me he meets my eyes with unabashed honesty. "I loved her with every part of me. She was my one, my only one. I would gladly have died for her and for you and Charlotte, but she wouldn't let me. She knew Hoyt would want you because you had inherited her gift. She was clearly the more powerful of the two of us, so she was the only choice to protect you, keep you from my brother." He smiles reminiscently. "Violet was fearless, at least for herself, a whole lot like you I'm betting. She wouldn't let any of the staff doctors touch her until the day you two were born."

"Why didn't she run before the births?" I ask.

"They didn't have a way to limit her powers, like you said they do now, and she probably could have." He smiles again in that distant way. "She was fierce, fought them as much as she could at every turn, but she didn't want to put you two at risk. Hurting you girls was the only thing that frightened her."

He sighs as though the weight of the world rests on his shoulders. "Vivian, it all began as an assignment—an assignment I didn't want, but it was so much more than that. In the end, she knew Hoyt would never hurt me, so she made me swear to take care of Charlotte, and as soon as she could travel, she took you and ran.

"She was going to send word to me at the facility somehow when she was well hidden. Neither of us could have guessed that Hoyt would allow, even help, me escape. But he wouldn't have if I'd kept you, and Violet had taken Charlotte. I know how insane this will sound to you, but I really believe he was making it up to me—making amends for some of the horror of what he was doing to us all.

"I couldn't wait for her message or for him to change his mind. You've seen his power and how easily he kills. Charlotte wasn't the asset he was after, so when he gave me an out, I took it. I left and prayed I'd see her again."

Taking a deep breath, he shakes his head. "A year went by, then two. Pretty soon I told myself to give up hope, but I couldn't extinguish it all, not until you showed up this afternoon. In the meantime, I had Charlotte to raise. I'm afraid I've done her an injustice, keeping her secluded here her whole life, never letting her experience too much of the outside world. I was even too afraid to send her to a regular school, especially after she manifested her power. My biggest fear has been that the Liaisons would find her and want her back despite my brother's influence."

His biggest fear is losing my sister? That shouldn't hurt, but it does. As far as he knew, she was his only living child; of course, that would be his biggest fear, but hearing him say it rips at my already jagged emotions. I turn away from him as my tears begin afresh.

"Sweetheart" —his low tone forces me back to face him—"I didn't know. If I had known that you had survived, I would have come for you, too."

"No, you wouldn't," I whisper. "That would have put Charlotte in jeopardy." It's harsh but true, and when he has the grace to glance away, I know I'm right. "But it's okay. I had Aunt Charlotte." Would she have gone after my sister had she known about her? Something tells me she would, but she had never seen Hoyt and the Liaisons at work firsthand. Harrison had. He knows the extent of their far-reaching influence and the power they wield at the hands of their recruits.

"How was it? Your life with Charlotte? Your mother talked about her nonstop. They were as close as sisters until, well"—he stops and shakes his head—"until I came along. Violet called home a few times, told her she was pregnant when we found out, and I always hoped they were reunited." He sighs. "At least she found a way to get the two of you together."

"Aunt Charlotte was my mom and dad. She was everything I needed before I knew I needed it." And I killed her, I add silently. "Did you choose Charlotte's name or did Violet?"

His brows draw together in disapproval. "*Your mother*"—he stresses the title—"chose both of your names right after you two were born."

Whoa, was that a reprimand? Is he actually going to give me grief about calling my mother by her name? Ignore it, Vivian. You don't have the energy tonight.

"How long were you together before she was taken away?" I ask, still stinging (but not sure why I am) from his disapproval.

He shifts uncomfortably and clears his throat, but before he can begin, the door opens, spilling light from the living room onto the porch. Charlotte steps out with an old school pipe, the kind Sherlock Holmes would light as he explains his genius to an amazed Watson.

"Thought you might want this, Dad," she says in her lilting voice.

"Thank you, honey." He pats her hand affectionately when he takes it and the small pouch she's carrying.

Charlotte glances quickly at me but turns abruptly and walks away before I can apologize for my shitty behavior. He packs the tobacco and lights the pipe. Pleasant cherry smoke wafts to me.

"Sorry, terrible habit, but one I can't seem to break. Don't actually want to truth be told, and that's what tonight's about. Truth," he says, leaning back against the post at his back. "Now, where were we? Oh yes, you asked about how long we were together." He inhales deeply and blows the smoke away from us. "We were a couple, a normal couple, for three months before Violet became pregnant. Happiest three months of my life. We did the usual couple things, went to the movies, out to dinner, planned our future together. I honestly believed I could escape from my brother and we could run away. If he asked my 'mission status,' I lied. I told him she was still uncooperative or that things were moving in the right direction. I think he knew, though. He knew how much she meant to me. Sometimes I would swear I'd see him, following us or spying on us, and when she told me about the pregnancy, I was overjoyed until I realized I'd given them exactly what they wanted."

"When did you tell that you had been assigned to seduce her?" I ask, leaning back.

He flinches, the pipe end glowing as he inhales again. "I guess I deserve that. But you have to understand, Vivian. I was trying to protect her. Hoyt was going to have her one way or another. He would have gone after her, taken her by force and tried to break her. She would have given birth to his children, not mine. Can you imagine what that would have been like for her? To give birth to the enemy's child? I didn't have much choice."

He sighs as he taps his pipe against the step, emptying it. "We fell in love, real love, and yes, she was terribly hurt when I told her, but after a couple of weeks, she forgave me. We made plans to run, but Hoyt came. I'm not even sure how he knew she was carrying. I had purposely had little contact since she told me of the pregnancy. While I was gone to buy supplies for our escape, he took her, and I had no choice but to follow. I wasn't going to leave her at his mercy."

"Was she happy? To be pregnant, I mean?"

"Yes, she was just like any other expectant mother most times. Neither of us tried to think too far into the future until near the end."

We sit quietly, he lost in the past, me in the present. Raking my fingers through my hair, I replay our conversation over in my mind.

"Wait, you said you hid Charlotte here because you were afraid the Liaisons would want her back. Why would they want her back? I thought I was the Gifted one."

"*You* are Gifted with your mother's power, and from what I saw tonight, mine as well, and you are definitely the more powerful of the two. That's usually the way with Gifted twins—just like with my brother and me. But Charlotte isn't without power. She didn't manifest for so long I doubted she had much at all." He shakes his head and raises his brows. "But when she did... I was blown away."

"Why? What can she do?" Maybe it's his tone, but for some reason tingles dance along my arms and down my spine. Wonderful, first I discover I'm going to have to share my father's affection, and now I have to share the spotlight, too. I try to push away my self-absorbed possessiveness, but it keeps hanging around like the smell of three-day-old fish. And it's just about as attractive, too.

"She has a power I've never seen, never even heard of," he says in awe. "She's a Twister of sorts."

"Oh, like Wyck or like Griffin?" I ask in relief. I've seen that trick. No biggie. She's not as special as he thinks.

"No, she doesn't reverse time or stop it. She can relive it," he replies.

"Like see the past in her mind?" Why is he so impressed by *that*?

He smiles. "No, she can travel back to the exact moment, see it while it's happening. It's as though she's *in* that moment with the people who experienced it. And she can take you with her."

Great. Hello, jealousy.

CHAPTER TWENTY-NINE

"YOU CAN STOP BEING so angry now, Vivian," Aunt Charlotte whispers, stroking a stray hair off my forehead. "You're home."

"No, this is not my home. My home is with you." I choke back a sob as she tucks the hair behind my ear. Her hands are so soft, too soft. She shakes her head, and red curls bounce.

"But I'm always with you," she says. "You can stop running."

"I can't. I can never stop. I was wrong to think I could." Tears slip silently down my cheeks.

"You can here, honey. You have everything you need right here." Her face begins to fade.

"NO! Don't go, Aunt Charlotte! I need you! Don't leave me again!" I reach for her, but she is less than mist; only her voice remains.

"No, you don't," she says as it drifts away.

*   *   *

Jerking awake, I inhale on a rush. Bright sunlight filters through the white curtains of Charlotte's room, illuminating every corner and a startled Petey lying close by my pallet on the floor. My eyes rove over the pine furniture and the multi-colored rag rug covering the hardwood floor, taking in the details I couldn't see last night when I'd tossed down my quilt and flopped on the unforgiving floor. Everything is perfect, like an ad for a cabin getaway. There aren't even dusty bunnies under the furniture. Figures.

"Don't!" Abby squeals then giggles from somewhere in the house. "Don't do that! You'll mess me up!" More giggles. More squeals.

I close my eyes, but reopening them doesn't change the room around me. Tossing the colorful quilt from my legs, I stand and stretch as smells of bacon and eggs waft in. I had absolutely not wanted to sleep in my sister's room and had set my foot down—on this hard floor by the way—when she'd been all helpy helperton and suggested we share her bed. At least Abby and the boys slept well guessing by the laughter and snatches of conversation I hear.

"Cooper, you're doing it wrong! Harrison said to stir it like this!" Abby exclaims.

So, it's 'Harrison' now. Wonderful. I'm so happy they are all super-fast friends. Maybe they will get matching BFF bracelets. I snarl in disgust as I pick up my quilts and pillow from the floor, tossing them onto Charlotte's already made bed.

On my way into Charlotte's half-bathroom, I trip over my bag and stub my toe on the door frame, which does nothing to improve my snarling. After taking care of morning business and twisting my hair into a sloppy bun, I slip on a blue t-shirt and jeans.

"How pathetic is this?" I ask, squatting in front of Petey who is eagerly waiting when I step out of the bathroom. "I'm reduced to befriending a dog—and not even my own dog." I rub his ears, and he snuggles into my hand before his floppy pink tongue licks my cheek. I scrub at the wet spot. "Hey, you, we just met. No kissing even if we did spend the night together." He nuzzles his big body against me, knocking me backward onto the floor.

"Does that go for me, too?" Standing in the doorway is Easton, unshaven and sleep-rumpled in only athletic shorts. Despite his deliciously-tousled appeal, my temper simmers.

"I'll have to think about that. And technically, you and I didn't spend the night together." I lurch to my feet, using Petey's broad back for support.

He arches a dark brow. "What's wrong with you this morning? Get up on the wrong side of the bed?"

"Yeah, the side that looks a whole lot like the floor, actually." I rub my back. "Feels a whole lot like it, too."

He leans one hand against the door facing, grins sinfully, and crooks his finger in a 'come hither' motion. And if I wasn't pissed at him for volunteering to sleep in the guest room with Wyck, I would oblige with a smile.

When I glare at him, hands akimbo, he steps into the room, making the size instantly shrink and my pulse quicken. "What is it?" He stops so close I can feel the heat from his body and smell his minty breath.

"I wanted"—my cheeks pinken, and I drop my eyes, embarrassed that I was about to admit how much I needed his comfort last night, to feel the weight of his calm as tangible as the weight of his arm across me—"I've gotten used to having you next to me, and... I just—" I sigh. "Never mind, I need some coffee that's all."

He lifts my chin, forcing me to meet his eyes. "I thought you might want a break, spend some alone time with your sister—that sounds so weird by the way," he says with another grin. When I don't return his expression, he leans in close and brushes his lips against mine.

"Truth is I *haven't* gotten used to you, babe. Being with you at night is a monster temptation. I think about that last night at the Shady Rest all the time. It's really hard to be so close to you and keep my hands to myself. Not to mention that this is your father's house. Insisting I share a room with his daughter is probably not a great first impression." He runs his fingertips lightly over my brows, my cheeks. "I know you need time to"—he looks around and rolls his eyes—"digest all of this, and I just thought you didn't need my kind of distraction right now." When his lips touch mine again, a voice from the doorway stops him.

"Wrong again, asshat. Distraction is exactly what she needs right now."

Wyck, completely dressed in khaki cargos and a red shirt, strolls in, side-steps Easton, and pulls my arm into the crook of his. "Princess, I would love to distract you right into the kitchen for some of Abby's surprisingly good breakfast." He sweeps the two of us past a none-to-pleased Easton. Over his shoulder, he tosses, "Don't you have a boy band audition somewhere?"

"You were eavesdropping?"

"Of course," he says, crinkling his forehead. "Somebody has to protect you from Mr. Pathetic." He shakes his head. "Honestly, he's a pretty sorry excuse for a guy. If I were him, I would have already—" Easton's hand on Wyck's shoulder stops his words but not his wiggling brow and bad boy smile. I laugh, and Wyck presses his hand against mine on his arm. But Easton knows he's only kidding and pushes him playfully—okay, maybe a little harder than that—grabbing my hand as we enter the kitchen.

Cooper and my father are seated at the table, half-empty plates in front of them, and Abby is spooning out scrambled eggs onto her own plate. Charlotte, wrench in hand, is tightening the faucet knobs. She glances back with a satisfied nod. When her gray eyes meet mine, she fidgets nervously before dropping her gaze and moving to an open toolbox on the counter. She replaces the wrench, closes the box, and walks out the opposite doorway without another look back.

My father, who's been watching this awkward interaction, tilts his head and raises his brow before saying, "Good morning, Vivian. Did you sleep well?"

With his question my severe mood comes roaring back. How can he act so normal this morning when I feel anything but normal? Even after our lengthy discussion last night, I still have oodles of questions. And on top of that, I have these feelings that I don't know how to handle. He claims to have loved my mom and not known I was alive, that he would have come for me had he known. The five-year-old inside of me wants to believe it all so much, but the seventeen-year-old is too jaded to allow it.

"Fine, I slept fine." I know my tone says otherwise. Retrieving a mug from the counter, I busy myself at the coffeepot, avoiding his gaze which follows me around the room until I'm seated next to Abby. She's devouring her breakfast at the table, looking adorable as ever with her glasses sitting low on her nose. She smiles sheepishly when she dribbles gravy onto her 'High Maintenance' t-shirt.

"I thought we might go for a group hike today. I've got a special treat for you all." He searches my face, but I only nod, watching Easton and Wyck fill heaping plates before joining us. He runs his hand through his hair. "Maybe you and I could talk some more?" he asks, leaning across the table and touching my hand where it rests on the mug. I nod again but glance at him, and he smiles warmly. He's obviously trying hard, and I know I'm acting like a jerk, but it doesn't stop me from pulling my hand back and leaving the table. Petey bounds through the door and pushes his nose against my knee.

"Should I take him out?" I ask without looking at my father.

"Yes, he hasn't left your side since he went into Charlotte's room last night. I think you've made a friend." The smile is evident in his tone.

Well, at least that's something.

"His leash is by the back door." He sips benignly from his mug as though it's business as usual at the Matthews's house.

Letting Petey lead the way, I finally exit the awkward father-daughter moment through the same doorway Charlotte used. I clip on Petey's leash and open the back screen door. The air chills my cheeks in that almost fall way. The dewy grass glistens in the early light, and I inhale until my lungs are full to bursting. Petey surges forward off the back porch, and I'm forced to follow as he, nose down, drags me toward the tree line not far from the house. His paws crunch in the undergrowth as he begins to pull me into the woods.

"Petey, no!" Charlotte exclaims from behind us.

Rising from an Adirondack on the porch, she points admonishingly at Petey. "Petey, you know you aren't supposed to go in there." I must have walked right past her when we came outside.

Petey, resigned to his limitations, does his business and heads back to Charlotte. She rises and steps inside but emerges in less than a minute with two bowls which she sets down on the porch steps. Petey dives into his food, and I'm forced to release him and climb the steps. I sit in the chair angled to face hers, a small wooden table between us.

"I didn't see you earlier," I say awkwardly because I don't know what else to say.

Her wheat-blonde hair practically glows in the morning sun as she nods her head. We both sit not looking at each other, nervously watching Petey as though he's a science experiment and we're waiting for him to explode or turn colors. Okay, I've got to say something to her, my sister. I've faced down a psycho killer *and* a self-possessed homecoming queen (who was almost as formidable). I can do this. I can begin a conversation with a girl who looks like my reflection and who's named after the most important woman in my life. Thinking of Charlotte brings back my dream. She said I had to stop running. Maybe this is what she meant.

"Wow, he must have been really hungry," I say. My need to pace has me fidgeting as though I'm sitting on an ant's nest.

She nods again. "He really likes this food, too." Her lilting voice is almost musical, reminding me of songbirds in spring.

"How often do you feed him?" I ask, not believing I'm really having a dialogue about the eating habits of a dog.

"Usually twice a day, but with all the excitement last night, I forgot." She chances a glance at me and smiles, the kind you give a stranger on the street, fitting though since that's what we are. "You can pace if you need to. It won't bother me." She nods toward the house. "I'm used to it."

My face must register my surprise at her knowing my thoughts because she quickly points to my legs and adds, "You can't sit still. That's the way Dad is, too." She laughs quietly, and as though her slip has embarrassed her, her cheeks turn the pink of a wild rose. In that moment, surrounded by the early-morning light, I begin to see the differences in our appearance rather than the similarities. Her soft features and shining hair are truly beautiful. Where I am often harsh and cynical, she is sweet and optimistic. I know this as surely as I know she's exactly the kind of person I wish I could be. No wonder our father sacrificed me for her.

Her smile, bigger this time, outshines the sun. "It's not twin power or anything. Don't worry. I'm not reading your mind."

"Can you? Can you read my mind?" I ask impulsively, suddenly wanting to know more about her.

"No, I'm not powerful like you." She shrugs. "I'm kind of a one-trick pony."

"Harris—our dad—told me a little about your abilities last night." Petey, mouth dripping from the water he's just slopped down, bounds onto the porch and stands between us, close enough for both of us to touch.

"Yeah, he says I'm a Twister. I don't really know much about the world of the Gifted. He's told me some, but I get the feeling he's holding something back." She strokes Petey's head. "Besides Dad, you're the only other Gifted person I've ever met."

"Not true." At her surprised expression, my reserve bends, and I smile at her. "Wyck is Gifted, too." Reaching out, I run my hand over Petey's back, still warm from standing in the sun. When she tilts her head quizzically, I nod. "In fact, you two have something in common. He's a Twister, not the same as you, but a Twister nonetheless."

"What can he do?" she asks, resuming her petting.

"He can stop time for a few seconds." Her eyes widen, and I continue. "Yep, I've seen it. In fact, he's saved my life a couple of times."

"I'd... I'd like to hear about that sometime." She shyly drops her eyes to Petey. When she does, her hand slides past Petey's head. For a brief second our fingers touch, and a jolt, not unlike what I felt the first time Easton and I touched in Mrs. Crafton's English classroom, races up my arm. She gasps, and we both jerk our hands back. She cradles hers against her chest.

Before either of us can really register what happened, Easton pushes open the screen door and steps onto the porch. "So, ladies, you ready to go on a hike?" He's grinning and sounds completely at ease.

Charlotte and I exchange a 'let's pretend that didn't happen' look as she rises, grabbing Petey's leash where it dangles still attached. Smiling timidly, she nods and allows Petey to lead her into the house.

Easton's brows draw together as he watches her retreating back. "What was that look about?"

Shaking my head, I stand and wrap my arms around his waist, pressing my cheek against his hard chest and inhaling that totally Easton smell. "Nothing. It's just weird, you know? We share so much but know so little about each other. We have the same DNA but not the same past." I hesitate. Do I tell Easton my real issue, that I'm so jealous of her life and her perfection I want to burst and take something with me in the process? I'm not sure anything will *ever* erase those feelings.

He returns my squeeze and rests his chin on the top of my head. "You need some time to get to know each other. Maybe this hike will help. I think we'll all feel more comfortable with each other after."

I want to agree, tell him I think it will. I want to believe it will magically take away my childish feelings. So, I nod because that's what he wants me to do, but somehow, I don't share his faith.

CHAPTER THIRTY

"I JUST LOVE THE WOODS," Cooper says for about the tenth time since we began this exhausting adventure. Even though the back of his grey shirt is sticking to him and wet with sweat, he's practically marching, a long stick in his hand like he's on a granola commercial.

Maybe that was my father's plan, wear us all out so I can't destroy anything else. We've been trudging through thick under-brush for hours. When the seven of us loaded with backpacks had first entered the tree line behind the house, the going hadn't been too bad. It had reminded me of camping with Aunt Charlotte, the trees, the sun, the smell of outdoors.

An unleashed Petey had run ahead, chasing squirrels and rabbits that always managed to escape and leave him puzzled. Charlotte seemed more human and less perfect, laughing with her—our—father. She even cozied up to Wyck during that first hour and stayed by his side. Though I couldn't hear their conversation, I had a feeling they were hitting it off. Wyck had smiled his devilish grin, and she had blushed furiously. Pretty soon they had fallen behind, and occasionally we had stopped to let them catch up.

But now, I'm exhausted. As the terrain began to climb steadily and the undergrowth became a tangled mass grabbing at my ankles, I lost my enthusiasm at the wonders of nature. My feet are sweaty inside my borrowed hiking boots, and my back is beginning to scream for a real rest even though Easton's carrying my backpack along with his. The thick canopy of leaves has protected us from the harshness of the noon sun but not from the foul mood beginning to creep in.

And when Coop once again exclaims how amazing this all is, I want to pummel him mercilessly with my remaining strength. Abby does it for me, whacking him across the arm.

"Hey! What was that for?" he exclaims, rubbing his upper arm.

"For being so excited!" She grabs one of the two backpacks he's carrying and successfully halts his progress, yanking out her water bottle. In a very non-Abby move, she drinks until it runs down her chin.

Harrison chuckles. "We aren't far now." He too stops for water and to allow Charlotte and Wyck to rejoin us. He lifts one brow at her as she approaches him.

"What?" she asks, making me wonder if we aren't a little more alike than I thought. "You don't have to wait, Dad. I can follow your trail. I'm not going to get lost." She huffs but drops her gaze, ruining her moment of defiance.

"I'm not worried about you getting lost." He glances with the same raised brow at Wyck, who has wisely chosen to stand next to Easton rather than joining Charlotte at our father's side. Wyck has the good grace to blush, surprising me. Wyck worrying about what a girl's dad thinks? She must have made a real impression, which shouldn't bother me. Wyck's affection was always a nuisance, but it was *my* nuisance, not hers. I should be glad he seems to like her, happy for both of them, but for some reason it seems as though she's taking yet another thing from me.

Drawing in a deep breath to calm myself into reasonability, I follow everyone else's lead and remove my water bottle, hoping to distract myself.

"Let's get going. I want to set up camp and catch our dinner before the sun goes down," Harrison says, taking Charlotte's empty water bottle and handing her his full one.

"Did you say catch our dinner?" Cooper's eyes light up. "As in fishin'? What are we waitin' for?" He pulls Abby to her feet. She squeals as he tosses her over his shoulder and spills most of her remaining water.

"Yes, exactly like fishing." Harrison smiles as he swings back into action.

Easton and I exchange a confused look. "Wait!" I yell.

Harrison turns back toward me.

"We're camping?" This does not sound good.

"Like, overnight? Outside? With the bugs and wild animals?" Abby adds, squirming down from her bottom-up position.

Harrison laughs, his green eyes the color of the leaves around us. "Well, that's usually how it works." Charlotte claps and jumps up and down ecstatically.

This day just keeps gettin' better. "Yeah, but camping 'usually' involves a tent," I snap, hands on my hips.

"You know, your mother once said almost the exact same thing, with that exact expression."

"Sounds like a smart woman," I mumble. But when he smiles like the love sick boy he must have once been, my smirking lips twitch into a reluctant half-smile.

"Oh, she was, and yes, camping definitely requires a tent. And fishing poles and flashlights and s'mores." He looks pointedly at Abby. "And bug repellent."

"You got a genie in that backpack?" I ask, a little less bitchy than a few minutes ago. He's really trying, and the least I can do is stop being a brat.

His smile broadens. "Nope, you only get three wishes with genies. I've got something better." At my raised brow, he turns and begins walking away. Over his shoulder, he calls out, "I've got a river."

"Well that makes loads of sense! Thanks for clearing that up!" I call out to his retreating back.

"O ye of little faith," he tosses back in a singsong voice.

Easton shrugs. Coop rubs his hands together greedily. Abby sighs. And Wyck practically skips to a bubbly Charlotte's side who takes the lead of our convoy of confusion.

"So, do you know what's going on?" Wyck asks, and I notice his hand brushes her as he swings his arm, lingering longer with each brush. I should probably stop watching.

"No, we've never been this far before," she says, her cheeks as flushed as a sunburn.

Wyck continues to brush his hand against hers until I can't take it anymore. "Wyck, stop being coy and just hold her hand already!"

Damn! What's wrong with me? When he looks back I try to play it off as a joke and smile, but his brows draw together as though he's afraid I'm about to sprout another head. At my shrug, he turns back to Charlotte, who is magenta, and for a second I'm scared she might spontaneously combust from embarrassment. Well, add that to the mile-long list of things to apologize for.

But Wyck takes my advice, and without looking at her, takes her hand in his. She smiles shyly but doesn't pull away, and except for the displeased expression on Easton's gorgeous mug, we continue on in relative peace until we reach a break in the trees.

Spread out before us is a grassy riverbank, and on it, a small, wooden boat filled with supplies. Fishing poles, tent poles, nylon bags, and a couple of frying pans nearly spill from its interior.

And Harrison, sitting on his backpack, is kicked back against a nearby tree.

"What the?" Abby's mouth is hanging open, and she stops so suddenly Cooper bumps into her, sending her stumbling forward a couple of steps.

Harrison spreads his arms wide. "Behold, ye doubters. Camping equipment."

"How did you—" I begin, but when he winks, I understand. "Of course, the river. You brought the boat here with your Gift." I nod. "Impressive."

"Dad, this is the boat we keep at the dock down from the house. You mean you made it travel all this way on its own?" Charlotte's eyes are the size of saucers.

"It wasn't hard, sweetheart. The river was never far from us all day, and I just gave tiny mental tugs to keep it moving." He shrugs. "I wasn't completely sure I could do it. It's been so long since I've done anything with my power. Guess it's like riding a bicycle. You never forget."

"But when did you pack the boat?" she asks as Cooper rushes forward, the gleam of a madman in his eye, to unpack the equipment. He grabs the fishing poles first. Easton and Wyck soon join him.

"Late last night after all of you went to bed. I figured this would be a nice distraction for everyone and give Vivian and me more time to get to know each other." He drops his arm around Charlotte. "Camping's one of our favorite activities." He looks at me. "I'm hoping it will be one of yours, too."

My throat tightens, and I'm forced to glance away to keep anyone from noticing how close to crying I am. He wants to be close to me.

He planned all of this for me, for us. I busy myself with taking off my backpack and joining the boys as they spread out all of the gear. Abby cops a squat beside Harrison, and Charlotte begins to gather small sticks to start a fire. It doesn't take long to set up the two tents (one for the guys and one for the girls) with all of us working together, and within the hour, Cooper is casting his line into the river. Easton and Harrison are in the woods, gathering wood for our fire, and Abby is stretched out on a blanket next to Coop, relaxing in the afternoon sun and actually smiling while Wyck and Charlotte work on the makeshift fire pit.

With no other distraction, my gaze is drawn to them like a magnet. Their heads are close together while they whisper and "accidentally" touch hands or brush arms. I feel that tiny twinge of jealousy that she has his attention, and I realize that I'm really scared I'll lose his friendship. We've grown so close since our stay at the facility, have so much in common, more than even Easton and I, and I'm terrified she'll come between our friendship. I have this irrational fear that he'll like her better than me.

Easton soon returns from his firewood expedition and throws down another load onto the stack not far from the pit. He swipes his shirt over his sweaty face. His dark skin glistens. He throws his shirt over a low-hanging tree branch and saunters toward me.

"Hope you're not planning on hugging me." I hold my nose. He grins wickedly.

"What's this? Vivian, the one who runs headfirst into any and every dangerous encounter she can find, is afraid of a little hard-earned sweat?" He plops down beside me and tackles me all in one gesture. I sound more like Abby when I let out a girly squeal.

"Yuck! Get off!" I push against his chest with the force that guarantees he'll win, and he tightens his arms around me in response. I laugh, and he smiles broadly.

"It's good to hear that," he says, staring down at me.

"What?"

"You laughing. I've been worried, babe. You always look so serious and unhappy lately."

"It's hard, finding my dad and getting her in the bargain." I nod my chin in Charlotte's direction.

His face becomes serious. "You wanted a family, right?" When I sigh, he smiles again and touches my cheek. "Just think of it as a bonus."

"A bonus? Is that supposed to be a joke?" The tension that had vanished with his approach suddenly slams me hard. My life, everything I know about myself, lies in ruins all around me and what's left standing is shaky at best, and Easton made a joke?

He raises his brows, his aqua eyes wide. "I didn't mean—look, I'm sorry. Don't overreact. I know it's hard, but—"

"You don't know anything about it!" When I push this time, it's with enough force to roll him off of me. "You have no idea what it's like! I've finally found my father after all these years only to find I have to share him with... with... Perfection Barbie, who's probably never even raised her voice much less killed someone! You have a family who loves you—a mom and a dad, but I have to force you to call them!" I leap to my feet, clench my fists at my side, and roar to the sky, all my frustration and jealousy in one fierce sound.

I don't dare look at any of them, doing instead what I do best. I run.

CHAPTER THIRTY-ONE

WHEN HARRISON FINDS ME, I've blown up a tree, exploded it like confetti. I unleashed on a poor, defenseless pine tree, and its smoking, charred remains are a reminder of my shame.

He doesn't say a word for what feels like hours. When he does speak, his reassuring voice amplifies my stupidity. "We have to stop meeting like this, sweetheart."

"How can you call me that when I've been nothing but an ass since I got here? What the hell's wrong with me?" I'm past tears, opting instead for self-loathing and pacing.

He laughs. The sound shocks me into stillness. "You're a super-naturally, extraordinarily Gifted teenage girl who just met her father and surprise twin sister." He shakes his head. "The teenage girl part alone would justify one exploding sink and" — he looks around — "one tree bomb."

But I can't return his good humor. "Why are you being so nice to me?"

His smile fades as he steps closer and takes my hand. "Vivian, I cannot imagine how hard this must be for you, how hard your entire life has been, and I'm your father. I want to help you even if that takes a few minor setbacks." He rubs my arm. "Would you rather I be mean? Angry because you're lashing out? Frankly, you're being mean enough for us both." He hugs me quickly but pulls away to meet my eyes. "Poor Easton looks a little like this tree right now." He motions to the smoldering pine stump behind him. "I think he can't decide if he's hurt or angry, most likely both. You need to stop hiding and fix this."

I only thought I was beyond tears as my vision swims. "He should leave. I would. I wouldn't have stayed this long." Panic clamps down on my heart. "I have to go talk to him before he takes off!" But when I try to sprint away, Harrison clamps down on my arm.

He smiles soothingly. "He won't leave and neither would you."

"How can you say that? I was so awful!" I try to break free, but his grip tightens.

"Yes, you were, but Easton could never leave you. It's quite surprising that you were able to leave him when your aunt was killed." At my puzzled expression, his brows draw together. "You don't know anything about your past do you?" When I don't respond, he inhales deeply.

"What past, like last spring?" I ask, shaking my head.

"Mr. Lewis didn't mention anything unusual about your relationship? I'm sure he felt the bond with his Magnet ability."

I think back to our last conversation in the diner. Mr. Lewis did mention something about the strength of our connection, but I haven't given it much thought. "He said our bond was old, beyond the present." I shrug. "But I have no idea what that means."

"Perhaps it's time you find out," Harrison says. He looks behind him, and for the first time I notice Charlotte semi-hiding behind a large oak tree. Oh, shit! What had I called her?

She steps timidly forward, but her eyes simmer gunmetal gray. She looks pissed. Good. Pissed I can deal with much easier than crying.

"Charlotte, I didn't see you—" I begin, about to apologize when she interrupts me.

"Yeah, you do that a lot, huh?" She motions around at the tree. "Must be easy to ignore other people *and their feelings* when you can do this."

Even Harrison is shocked. "Charlotte," he warns.

"No, she's right. You're absolutely right, Charlotte. I've been horrible to you, and I'm really sorry. I can't honestly promise I won't ever say or do something terrible ever again, but I feel really bad about hurting you and calling you that name."

She still looks angry but not quite so murderous. "I'm not perfect, Vivian. I'm nothing compared to you." I try to interrupt her, but she holds up her hand. "No, let me finish. You have amazing abilities. You're obviously smart and confident. You can take care of yourself. I could never do the things you've done. So, whatever it is you're feeling toward me is dumb. I'm just a girl." Her face softens when she smiles awkwardly, nervously, waiting for my response.

I sigh. "I'm sorry. I truly am."

Harrison pulls us both into his arms, nearly banging our heads together. He releases us and nods at Charlotte. "Honey, I think it's time to show Vivian what you can do. Show her Virginia."

CHAPTER THIRTY-TWO

"WHO'S VIRGINIA?" I ask as Harrison motions me to sit on the ground.

"Your past. Now sit. You shouldn't be standing your first time. You may get dizzy." He kisses Charlotte on the forehead. "Don't be nervous. Concentrate. I know it was a long time ago, but you can do it again." She nods and sits facing me.

"Will one of you please tell me what's going on?" I ask as Harrison kneels down next to me and puts his hand on my shoulder.

"Charlotte is going to take you into the past. You won't be physically leaving. Your body will stay here, safe and sound, so don't be afraid. She's going to show you the origin of your power and explain your connection to Easton in the process. She showed me several years ago after reading an old journal I stole from the files the Liaisons kept on your mother and her family. You won't be able to use your Gift, but you won't need to. No one will see you or hear you." He kisses my forehead as he had Charlotte's, and I'm momentarily thoughtless until he smiles. "Charlotte won't let anything happen to you."

"Close your eyes," Charlotte says, taking both of my hands in hers. "Try to relax and clear your mind."

I concentrate on the softness of her hands and the sound of my breathing. Within minutes I'm no longer surrounded by the sounds and smells of the forest. I'm in a kitchen, an old kitchen. A young woman in a white gown is poking futilely at a pitiful fire in the hearth. Her mouth moves, but I can't hear her words.

Charlotte's voice startles me, and I jump. "We won't be able to hear anything, like watching a movie on mute. These really old visits are hard, but I can tell you the story as we go along since I've read St. Clair's journal. St. Clair was a wealthy land owner in the Colonies. This is his house." She points to the young woman who seems to be searching for something. "That's Virginia." The lightning outside illuminates her striking gray eyes.

"Her eyes," I whisper even though I remember Harrison telling me they won't hear me.

"Yeah, guess that's a family trait, too." Charlotte tugs gently on a strand of my hair that's slipped loose from the hairband. She points to the girl, and I notice her long, brown braid swinging down her slim back. When she turns around with a cup in her hand, I glimpse for the first time her rounded belly. She caresses it lovingly as she speaks.

"Virginia is pregnant with Robert's baby, but there are a few problems with that." She ticks off the first one on her fingers. "Number one, Robert's St. Clair's son. Robert is above her station, and even though she thinks he will take care of her, she is tragically mistaken. Number two"—she holds up a second finger—"Robert is away in England picking up his new bride." She shakes her head. "Poor girl, she has no idea. Number three, Virginia's been drinking some kind of herbs prepared by a woman the villagers claim is a witch. It helps her aches and pains from the baby and all the work she's forced to do. She wouldn't need it if that old hag who runs the house wasn't working her so hard."

Lightning flashes brighter than before, and Virginia bends at the waist, grasping her stomach, right before she hits her knees. The cup's blue liquid spreads across the floor. She is silently screaming. A young man bursts through the door and rushes to her.

"Enter Ethan. Ethan is another servant in the house, and I'm pretty sure he's in love even before their uniting—you'll see that later." The shirtless boy with dark hair and a form shaped from strenuous labors lifts her tenderly while she cries. Another door opens and a gray-haired old man shouts at the pair, oblivious to the rain soaking the floor and him.

"Is that St. Clair?" I ask, not bothering to whisper this time.

"Yes, he was some sort of mad scientist, doing all kinds of weird experiments. Everyone thought he was crazy, and he proves them right years later. He founded the Liaisons."

My stomach turns as I stare at the man who is responsible for so much pain and death. My anger rises, and I'm about to blast him when I realize, I'm powerless, no blue, no surge, nothing. I remember Harrison telling me I wouldn't be able to use my Gift here, and it's lucky for St. Clair I can't.

"You want to hurt him. I know. Dad nearly cried when he discovered he couldn't do anything on this side," Charlotte explains. "Oh! Here comes the hag."

A split second later an enormous woman fills the doorway through which Ethan had arrived. After several minutes of shouting, Ethan brushes past St. Clair and out into the storm.

"What's happening? Is it over?" I ask anxiously, not ready to go back yet.

"No, change of scenery, though." She follows Ethan into the wet night, but we remain dry, as though an enormous umbrella shelters us. "The old hag is the housekeeper, and she won't allow Virginia to give birth in the house because of the herbs from the witch lady. So, Ethan is taking her to St. Clair's workshop, and that's where the magic happens." She grins excitedly. "I love this part!"

We follow Ethan inside a cavernous building filled with glass containers of all shapes and sizes and filled with liquid—very Frankenstein's lab. He lays her gently on a large wood and metal table with odd rods that touch the ceiling.

"What kind of experiments was this freak doing?" I attempt to touch one of the rods, but my hand ghosts through it.

"We can't interact," Charlotte says, "just watch. St. Clair wanted to live forever. He was into all kinds of freakish things."

We watch as Ethan tries to make Virginia more comfortable by placing a coat beneath her head. His eyes plead desperately with her, holding her fisted hand and stroking her cheek. The two of them together might as well be Easton and me (without the whole baby thing). The way he touches her, the way he loves her.

"That's our connection, isn't it?" I turn to Charlotte. "We're them. They're us. Destined to be together always."

"That's what Dad and I think. We talked about it this morning before anyone else was up. When you two showed up together, it was so obvious. I mean, look at them. You guys even sort of look like them, and you said it was strange how Easton just found you working in a diner in the middle of nowhere. He has to be with you. It's fate."

Mr. Lewis sensed it, and Hoyt must have, too. He used our connection to find me, so he must have known.

When St. Clair reappears, gesturing and yelling, Ethan steps close to him, the way guys do when they want to establish the pecking order. In less than a minute, St. Clair moves to the end of the table while Ethan fetches a bucket for St. Clair.

"There's so much blood." I'm whispering again but this time from disbelief that any woman, especially one so fragile, could survive that much blood loss.

"Yeah, if not for the lightning, she and the baby would probably have died," Charlotte whispers back.

Virginia bolts upright with a strength I wouldn't have guessed she had and grabs the metal pole with her right hand. With a loud boom and brilliant flash, electricity races down the pole, into Virginia's hand and through Ethan. Virginia, Ethan and the baby create a circuit. A familiar blue light fills the room, pinpointing to one spot, Virginia's right hand where it still grips the pole.

We watch as St. Clair delivers a baby girl. When the workroom begins to fade from view, Virginia and Ethan are smiling down on her.

"Open your eyes, Vivian," Harrison says.

Charlotte is smiling, wiping her hands on her jeans. "Sorry, my hands got sweaty." She motions to my own hands which are still out in front of me where she was holding them. I turn them over, marveling at how with only a touch she was able to take me back hundreds of years to literally see the birth of my power!

"How? Why?" I ask both of them.

"I think it was a lot of things." Harrison helps Charlotte to her feet. "From all I've read in St. Clair's records and journals, he spent the rest of his days tracing Virginia and her children then he went after others. He searched the globe for Gifted people and persuaded them, sometimes by force, to join his group. Then he began selling their services to the highest bidder. He proposed that the herbal mixture Virginia was drinking had some sort of magic in it."

"Magic? You don't really think the woman who was making the mixture was a witch, do you?" I snort skeptically.

"That's the part of this story you find hard to believe?" Charlotte, a hint of a smirk on her full lips, holds out a helping hand to me.

"Good point." She nods.

"Stranger things have happened, sweetheart." Harrison picks up a piece of the charred wood chips and holds it up. "As I was saying"—he looks pointedly at the two of us, telling us without words to stop interrupting—"I think it was the herbal drink and the lightning working together. Combine those two with Ethan's determination that Virginia and the baby would live, and abracadabra! The recipe for a Gift." He puts the wood chip in his pocket and smiles thoughtfully. "A memento of an important day."

"Well, I'm going to head back, Dad, if that's okay. I want to help with supper." She ducks her head shyly, and Harrison and I both know what she really wants is to see Wyck.

Harrison grunts, displeasure on his face for the first time since he found me wallowing in self-inflicted idiocy. "I'll be right behind you, honey," he replies then mumbles, "close behind you."

I smile, really smile, at such a normal family. "You coming back soon?" Charlotte asks me.

"Yeah, but I have something I need to do first, that is if I can find Easton. I want to apologize and tell him how much I love him and need him."

"Oh, I'll bet you find him." She winks. "After all, you've had hundreds of years of practice."

As she moves to leave, I call out to her. "Charlotte"—she turns, a question on her face—"you are way more than just a girl. Thank you."

Her smile lights up the darkening forest. "You're welcome, sister."

CHAPTER THIRTY-THREE

Reclaimed

In my hand,
I hold coordinates,
coordinates to my
past
and my
future.
For eleven years,
I have felt her
but couldn't find her.
For eleven years,
I have relived that night.
It has to happen
sooner
or later
I told myself
every morning,
every evening,
every mission.
Sooner or later,
she will emerge.
She is too powerful.

The cause will have its weapon yet.
Unstoppable.
Untouchable.
Victorious.
Every day without her
is a day without the missing part
of myself.
I will bring her here
and with her,
I will lure him back.
His bitterness will fade.
He will forgive me
when he sees she is alive.
He will be my brother again.

CHAPTER THIRTY-FOUR

BY THE TIME I FIND EASTON, darkness has set in. Water drop-lets cling greedily to his hair, glistening diamonds in the nearly-full moon. He is chest deep in the river; his clothes and a towel lie on the bank where the grass changes to sand. I pull back into the shadows, watching like a lecher.

Are we really meant to be, like Ethan and Virginia? Is that why we've always had this connection between us? My head says it isn't possible, but is anything I've experienced in the last six months possible?

He submerges and surfaces several feet away before he swims parallel to the shore, against the current. He's struck a furious pace, and I know he's trying to work out his anger at me, replace his burning fury with burning muscles.

My face heats, and my heart races watching his shoulders bunch as he glides through the water. When he stops, he's breathing heavily. He trudges closer to the bank, sliding his hands through his hair. When the water is waist deep, he slams his fists down hard on the surface.

"Dammit, Vivian!" he shouts.

For a second I think he's seen me lurking in the dark, but he looks up to the starry sky and shakes his head.

"Easton!" I yell.

I step out of the shadows and rush toward him, uncaring that my clothes will be soaked. As I slosh noisily through the water, he whips around to catch me, stumbling back a step. Despite the chilly water or maybe because of it, I'm acutely aware of his warm body pressed against mine.

"I'm so sorry, Easton! I screwed up again! I love you, and I don't deserve you!" I squeeze him so tightly he grunts, but finally, he wraps his arms around me. He pulls back and stares down at me, not saying a word for so long I get nervous that he's going to reject me.

"You're lashing out at the people who love you, Vivian. First Wyck and now me. You have your family, the father you wanted and a sister. Is it the way you expected? No, but you did it, babe. You found your father, and he obviously loves you."

I open my mouth to agree with him, tell him that he is absolutely right, but he holds up a dripping hand.

"Let me finish. Charlotte was a surprise to all of us, and I can't imagine how hard that must be for you, but you're acting immature and ridiculous. You just met them. You have to give it time. And I'm not goin' anywhere no matter how hard you push me away."

"But you have a life. You should be starting college in less than a month, and your parents need you. I don't want to be the one who keeps you from them." I glance down at the dark water between us, feeling as though it's an entire ocean. "I don't want to turn into a regret years down the road." My fingers tighten on his shoulders in fear that he'll actually take my advice and leave me.

"I've told you before, *you* are my family. Once you're settled in, whether here or somewhere else, I'll go home, pack the rest of my things, and come back to you. I can go to college anywhere." He cups my cheek. "When are you going to understand that I can't be apart from you? It's not physically possible."

He shakes his head. "It sounds completely crazy, but before we met, I always felt like something was missing. That's why I played baseball. I tried every sport, thinking I could fill the gap or at least make it seem smaller, but it never worked. That day in English... I can't explain it, but I felt so... relieved, like I could finally breathe."

He's my Ethan. He's my forever. Before he can say another word, I put my hand on the back of his head and pull his mouth to mine. It's been so long since we've been truly alone that we kiss as though we're starving for each other, devouring with a kiss. It doesn't take long for the kiss to become more, and when he presses me to him, I become very aware that his clothes are on the riverbank.

He pulls my t-shirt over my head and tosses it on the bank where it lands with a soggy thud. His hands slide over my back, and my bra follows my shirt. My already messy bun tumbles down when his hands reach my hair. With every breath, I inhale him; with every touch the energy tingles between us until it seems we're both glowing from it.

His lips trace my neck, my collarbone, before finding their way back to mine. His hands span my waist then glide upward until I'm breathless. He groans my name against my ear then swings me easily into his arms, water-logged shoes and all, and carries me to the bank. When he sets me on my feet again, instinctively, I wrap my arms around my chest to cover myself while he unfolds and spreads the big beach towel lying next to his clothes.

I'm trying (and failing) not to watch his naked body bending and flexing. I've never seen a guy without clothes, so I don't really have a reference point here, but he looks completely perfect, all long, lean muscle and tan skin, lighter where his clothes normally are, and totally male. His powerful hands smooth the oversized towel as gently as his hands caress my skin.

He turns around and catches me looking. My cheeks flame, but he only smiles his seductive little half-grin and stands unmoving for a minute, then my cheeks really burn.

He kneels at my feet, and I brace my hands on his shoulders as he removes my boots and socks, sliding his hands up my jeans to the waistband when he's finished. He pauses at the button and peers up at me as if silently asking my permission. At my nod, he pulls down my pants but leaves my wet underwear behind, a final barrier to the act my body is screaming to experience.

His lips find mine again, gently this time, and we both tremble. Knowing that he's just as nervous and excited as I am increases my need, and I slide my arms back around his neck, holding him tightly to me as he steps backward on the towel.

When we're lying next to each other, I realize this is it. I'm not hesitant or unsure anymore. *This* is my perfect moment, the one Easton wanted for me at the Shady Rest. He wanted my first time, our first time, to be perfect. Nothing could be more perfect than moonlight, the soft sounds of the forest close by, and the boy who crossed eternity to find me.

* * *

"Why are your clothes all wet?" Abby asks. She and the others, holding sticks with marshmallows perched at the end, are gathered around the small fire.

I'm sure my cheeks give away what we've been doing. Embarrassment makes me fidget and stammer, so Easton, smiling slyly, rescues me. "She fell in the river while we were goofin' around."

Abby laughs. "You're so clumsy sometimes, V. Come sit next to me so you can dry out." She pats a spot on the blanket beside her.

Cooper and Wyck exchange a look across the flames then both grin knowingly, causing my already red face to feel like it's going to burst into flames. Did I mention how glad I am it's dark?

"Here, honey," Harrison offers, removing his button-up shirt, revealing a white t-shirt beneath. "You can change in one of the tents. There are some blankets in there, too."

"Be right back," I mumble, tripping on a piece of firewood in my rush to find the safety of the tent.

Minutes later I emerge from the tent, my father's shirt hanging to my knees and a blanket wrapped around my shoulders. When I take my wet clothes to a tree limb outside the range of the fire's light, Easton hurries from his seat next to Abby to help me. Our hands brush, and heat rushes through me, causing my hand to instantly glow. He smiles and kisses my forehead.

"Have I ever told you how adorable you are when you're embarrassed?" he whispers close to my ear so the others, who've grown nosily quiet, won't hear.

I try hard to meet his eyes and smile confidently, like a modern woman who doesn't worry about that awkward 'after the big deed' feeling. But truth be told, I'm not feeling at all cool and collected; I'm actually feeling the exact opposite.

Our time together was so wonderful. It seemed like the world was one of those twinkly stars above us, and we were in our own universe for just a little while. Coming back to reality... way harder than my choice to be with Easton. I don't regret my decision. I'd make the same choice right now. I'm just not sure how he feels. He's obviously happy, and he's being really sweet and attentive, but I'm still tempted to enter his mind and read his thoughts.

When I don't reply, he bends down, making himself eye level with me and forcing me to look at him. "Hey, what's wrong? You don't wish we hadn't..." he trails off, lifting his brows. Misreading my silence, he quickly adds, "Did I hurt you? You said you were alright, but—" he shakes his head, his expression worried and nervous.

"No, Easton, it's nothing like that." I sigh. "I guess I'm feeling kind of"—I shrug—"vulnerable or something. How do you feel about what happened? Do you wish we'd waited?"

"No!" He says loudly before dropping his voice to a whisper again. "No, I couldn't be happier, babe. Why? Do you?" he asks, his brows drawn tightly together over his aqua eyes.

I smile shyly and relax. He's as insecure about it as I am. "No." I touch his face while gripping my blanket tightly in one hand. "No matter what happens from here on out, I will never regret it." He exhales loudly and smiles, too, and I can't resist teasing him. "Although I *am* a little surprised you were so well prepared for our unexpected activity. Don't get me wrong. I'm glad, but very surprised considering it wasn't exactly planned."

I'm rewarded when his handsome face turns red enough to make his olive cheeks pink. "It's a guy thing, babe, an essential part of every guy's wallet. Ya know, always be prepared." He hitches one shoulder and grins.

"I thought that was the Boy Scout motto?" I poke him in the ribs.

He squirms. "What'd you think they meant by that?" He laughs loudly at my mock outrage when I slap him gently on the arm. I turn toward the others, but he pulls me back into his arms and the shadow cast by the tree.

"Seriously, Vivian, I wouldn't take it back either. And it only makes what I feel about you stronger, so no regrets, okay? I won't pressure you. It doesn't have to happen again if you don't want to." His serious expression is nearly painful.

I stand on tiptoe, sliding my free hand into his hair, and nip his bottom lip, satisfied by the sound that escapes on his exhale. He slips his arms around my waist, his reaction totally undermining his celibate declaration. Gliding along his rough cheek, I whisper breathily into his ear. "I don't think you have to worry about that." I kiss the sensitive spot just beneath his earlobe, and his grip tightens.

"Good, because I was gonna drown myself in that cold ass river if you'd gone along with that suggestion." He groans, breathing heavily. Just as his hands slip beneath my blanket, Abby calls out.

"Hey, get a room you two!" She begins to laugh then stops. "Oh, sorry, Harrison. That was, like, inappropriate, huh?"

"What's worse, Abby making raunchy comments or Vivian making out in the dark with the asshat?" Wyck asks.

Easton sighs loudly. "He's such a dick." He shakes his head. "I'm really gonna hate myself for what I'm about to say, but he's right. We should go back."

I slide back down his chest, making sure to press solidly against him, eliciting another of those delicious sounds from deep in his throat.

"What took you two so long?" Cooper asks with a wink as we settle onto one of the blankets.

"Didn't want Vivian to have wrinkles in her clothes." Easton says smoothly, nodding to the pan of fish which Coop passes over to him.

Using his fingers, he picks the flaky, white meat from the bones and hands me pieces between bites of his own while the others laugh and talk around us. I glance across the fire at Charlotte, who is openly holding Wyck's hand. He catches my gaze and smiles broadly. In my head, I hear his voice.

Thank you for bringing me along, Princess.

I mouth, "Anytime."

My father pats Charlotte's knee as he tells a story about how she was once chased through their backyard by a ferocious squirrel, and I laugh, too, imagining her blonde pigtails flapping.

Easton sets down the pan and drops his arm around my shoulders. This family thing might all work out after all. A wave of immense contentment sweeps like a wind through me followed immediately by a severe case of the goose bumps that have nothing to do with the temperature. Life is a tradeoff. Everything comes with a price, and I can't for one second 'good feeling' myself into thinking I'm finished paying.

CHAPTER THIRTY-FIVE

SLEEPING IN A TENT is everything I remember it being—uncomfortable. The only redeeming thing about the long, restless night was having Abby and Charlotte there. We spent most of the night telling Charlotte stories of Trista Parmer, our high school nemesis, and Hoyt and his cronies, our current nemesis. While reminiscing emphasized just how much Abby and the others mean to me, it also emphasized how desperately I want them all to be safe.

When the morning sun heats our tent, we shed our sleeping bags and stumble groggily out. After dressing in my stiff but dry (and unwrinkled) clothes, Abby and I watch as Charlotte washes, retrieves bacon and eggs from the big cooler, and begins breakfast while the men are still sleeping.

"You two can go wash up if you like," Charlotte says cheerily.

"You sure? We could stay and help," Abby replies. I lift one brow. Since when did Abby become so domestic and eager?

Charlotte shakes her head. "The boys and Dad should be up soon."

Grabbing a towel to share, we head downstream. Walking so close to the river reminds me of Easton, and a full-body flush creeps along my body. I smile thinking of his kiss, his hands, his—

"So, what do you think of her?" I'm so deep in my lustful memories that Abby's question makes me jump. She stops walking and draws her head back quizzically. "Jumpy?"

I smile. "I was thinking about the hike back." I lie. I'm not quite ready to share *everything* with Abby just yet.

"I like her, I think. It's just so weird, Ab. One minute I have no family, the next I have a father and a twin." We stop and kneel next to the river to splash water on our faces. I figure this is as good a time as any to bring up why she needs to go home. "Abby, you know school starts back really soon."

"Ugh! Don't remind me," she says, wiping her face with the towel.

I take a deep breath. "I think you should start home soon, like tonight or tomorrow."

Surprisingly, she doesn't look like she's going to argue. Instead, she sighs and glances away. "Yeah, I know. I've been thinking about it since we got here. I spoke to my parents before we left for the hike. They're coming home in a couple of days, and they're, like, feeling all 'parenty' or some crap. They want to spend some time with me before school starts. But I don't want to leave you, V. How will I ever make it in that hell hole without you there by my side?"

I pat her shoulder then pull her into my arms. "Oh, Abby, things will be different this year. You're a senior." I shoot for an excited tone without quite reaching the mark. "We always dreamed of senior year." I'm trying to make her feel better, but I don't believe it myself.

"Yeah, right. You're gone, Coop's gone, and Easton's gone. Just thinking about going back makes me sick. And you keep pushing me to go." She sobs against me, her shoulders shaking.

"I don't mean it like that. I'm not trying to push you to go." I pause, recalling how many times I've told them all to go home. "Okay, maybe I have but only because I want you safe. I'm with my father now, and you have to go back to school."

"I don't have to." She sniffs loudly and runs her palm across her nose. "I could get my GED like you did, and Cooper and I could stay here. Get our own place." When I start shaking my head, she only talks louder. "It would be great! My parents are never home; they wouldn't even know I was gone for a good month or two!" She smiles sadly.

I start to tell her how crazy that idea is, but she's probably right. She'd be better off here than home with parents who barely know her. Sighing, I touch her hand. "I can't make your decisions for you, but promise me you'll go home for a little while anyway."

It's all I can really ask of her after all she's done for me and with me over that last couple of months, over the last twelve years. She's faced nearly as much as I have and without the benefit of a supernatural power.

Her smile widens, and she hugs me tightly. "I promise."

"Sunshine, where are you?" Cooper calls loudly as he walks toward us.

"I'm over here, Cooper!" Abby exclaims. "Oh, V, I'm so excited! I've got to tell Cooper my idea." She laughs as she scurries away. She leaps into his arms when she reaches him, wrapping her legs around his waist and squealing.

I hate to hurt her, but I'm never going to stop trying to talk her into staying away until Hoyt is gone. Then again, he could go after her even at home because he knows I'll always protect her. I jab my hands into my tangled curls. Will nothing ever be easy again? Watching my reflection ripple in the water, I wonder what it would be like to be a normal senior, going to bonfires by the lake, decorating for homecoming dances, drinking hot chocolate at football games. But then I realize I wouldn't have done those things anyway. Abby and I were never on the inside; we were ostracized and bullied because we chose not to be like the others. But if I had it to do over, would I do it the same?

Easton's reflection appears behind me. His expression turns grim when he sees my face. "What is it? What's wrong, babe?" He kneels beside me.

My smile is half-hearted. "Thinking about senior year." His brows draw together in confusion. "What senior year is supposed to be anyway." I stand, and he follows.

"Why?" he asks.

I wave my hand to dismiss the whole thing. "I was trying to convince Abby to go back home. It's nothing." I loop my arm through his as we walk back to camp together.

"I'm sorry, babe," he says, voice as downcast as his eyes.

"Sorry? For what?"

"You're missin' out on a lot of things, and I wish things were different for you."

"Like what? Getting called names at lunch or being assaulted in the cafeteria?" I snort humorlessly, playing off my earlier sentimentality.

"Things would have been different this year. After what you did to Trista, I have a feeling things would be *very* different." He shrugs and smiles.

I giggle thinking of the look on Trista's face after I brainjacked her at prom last spring. "I've got a feeling you might be right."

* * *

After breakfast, we all help pack the supplies back into the small boat, strap on our packs, and head off into the woods. As we're leaving, I turn to see the boat drifting slowly on its way as if being pulled by a magic string with Harrison standing close by on the shore. He turns to see me watching him and smiles warmly.

"Should beat us back," he says. He rubs my shoulder affectionately then turns serious. "I really hope you're planning on staying with us, Vivian. You're a part of this family, and Charlotte and I really want you with us."

I nod. "I think I'd like that."

"Good," he says with another smile before putting his arm around me.

The hike back is pleasantly quiet and surprisingly relaxing. By the time we get back to the house, it's late afternoon, and though we're all tired, it's a good kind of tired. When we emerge once again in the backyard, Petey barks excitedly. He stands unmoving just inside the ring of trees that create a natural fence.

"Guess he's glad to be home, too. Come on, boy. I'll get you something to eat," Charlotte says. But Harrison's brows draw together as he tilts his head.

"Wait," he says ominously. "I don't think so. Wait here." He looks pointedly at me then moves cautiously toward the house, Petey running ahead of him.

A sick feeling settles in my stomach as Easton takes my hand, and Wyck moves closer to Charlotte. Before Harrison reaches the porch, Griffin steps around the corner of the house. Wyck's jaw clenches.

"Who's that?" Charlotte asks. When she steps forward, Wyck pulls her back.

"Stay here," he commands as he walks toward the opening in the trees.

I look at Easton, and he nods as I quickly follow Wyck into the yard. At his outraged expression, I shake my head. "So not happening."

"Who are you?" Harrison asks as we approach from behind him. When we're standing on either side of him, he raises his brows at me in silent question.

"He's my brother," Wyck answers, his jaw tight and his eyes glued to Griffin as he steps in chest-to-chest with him. "How did you find us?" His navy eyes burn with undisguised fury.

My eyes scan as much of the yard and house as I can see while I reach out with my mind, searching for Hoyt. If Griffin's here, the others can't be far behind.

"How do you think?" Griffin asks quietly. His body doesn't radiate the same intensity as Wyck's, his eyes darkened by sadness, not anger.

"Hoyt." Wyck snorts and shakes his head. Harrison tenses, and he too begins to search the surrounding area for the brother he hasn't seen in so many years. "Where are the others?" Wyck turns his head from side to side, looking behind Griffin's still form in an exaggerated motion. "I don't see them, but I know you aren't brave enough to face me without them, especially not after our last visit."

Griffin pales and touches his left brow where I notice for the first time a tiny pink scar marring the angelic perfection of his face. He must have gotten that when Wyck kicked his ass in the cemetery.

"I'm alone." His voice is so low I can barely hear him. "I haven't come to fight, Wyck."

"Oh, I know that, Griff. You're obviously suicidal to show up here alone. I would have killed you that day if it hadn't been for your buddies, and I swore to myself I'd finish the job if I ever saw you again." Wyck's face contorts into a mask of unrepentant revenge, and I know he's telling the truth. He won't stop this time. I won't be able to stop him.

"You're my brother." Griffin reaches out and touches Wyck's shoulder, and that's the catalyst to Wyck's fury. He pushes Griffin, full-force in the chest, then leaps on top of him, pinning Griffin's arms and body to the ground.

"You don't get it, do you?" Wyck yells, jerking Griffin up by the front of his shirt until they are nose-to-nose. "We aren't brothers anymore! We haven't been brothers since you let them kill our mother!" He shakes him violently until Griffin resembles a bobble head.

Harrison and I spring at them. We both pull at Wyck's arms, trying to yank him off of Griffin before he follows through with his threat, but Wyck's determination is too strong. I don't want to hurt him, but I have no choice. I'm not going to let him live with his brother's blood on his hands.

Releasing him, I step back, readying to hit him with a blast strong enough to knock him backwards and off of Griffin. But just as I'm raising my palm, footsteps pound the ground behind us. Easton and Cooper join Harrison, and their combined strength is enough. They all tumble back and fall hard on their behinds with Wyck held securely in Cooper's bear hug embrace.

"Let go, Cooper! Stay out of this—all of you! He knew about our parents! He knew!" Wyck stops fighting and drops his head. His shoulders begin to shake. "He knew," he sobs, crying freely and shocking all of us.

Charlotte rushes to his side, and Cooper releases him into her arms. Wyck wraps himself around her, dwarfing her tiny frame.

Griffin hoists himself to a sitting position. He's breathing harshly and holding his head as though he's trying to assure himself it's still intact. "Thank you," he says glancing over at me.

"I didn't do it for you." I lower my hand. "And if you try anything, I won't hesitate to finish what he started."

He shakes his head as he stands. "I didn't come here to fight, Vivian." His voice sounds much older and sadder than when I first met him only a few months ago, like he's aged twenty years. Gone is the overly-enthusiastic boy who so loved Lilah's jungle image that day in the practice facility. The man before me is jaded and tired, all sparkle missing from his eyes.

"Then why are you here?" Easton asks.

"I'm here to warn you. They know you're here." His eyes scan the group before coming back to me.

Wyck pulls back from Charlotte, his tears exhausted, but he doesn't remove his arm from her waist. "They?" He stands, bringing Charlotte with him. "You're one of them, Griffin. How do we know you aren't the first-round distraction?"

Griffin sighs. "I overheard the commander making plans with Ferguson and Lilah. I was left out. He doesn't trust my loyalty anymore," he says hanging his head. "He doesn't know I'm here."

"The golden boy finally came to his senses?" Wyck snarls sarcastically.

But Griffin ignores him. "You have to leave." He looks at me. "Especially you."

Harrison puts his arm around my shoulders like he did in the forest. "Let my brother come. No one's going anywhere. This is Vivian's home now."

I remember the dream I had of Aunt Charlotte, how she kept telling me I could stop running. "I'm finished running, Griffin."

"But he's back to his full power. You can't stop him, not with Lilah, Ferguson, and Zeb."

"We did it before," Wyck sneers, moving closer to his brother again.

Easton steps between them and puts his hand on Wyck's chest, but it's Griffin he stares down. "Thanks for the warning, but Vivian's right. We're through running away from him."

"They're safer here with our combined Gifts than anywhere else," Harrison says.

"Really?"

Our heads turn in unison to see Lilah's image shimmer into focus behind Griffin. She's only a projection, like before, but she's so vivid that I can see the sparkles on her short, black skirt.

Griffin's jaw drops. "Lilah?"

She rolls her eyes. "Very good, genius."

Wyck throws aside Easton's hand and pushes closer to Griffin. "Thought you said you came alone."

Griffin's eyes grow wide as he shakes his head in surprise. "I didn't know she was coming! I swear it!"

I quickly search his mind. "He's telling the truth, Wyck."

Lilah laughs cruelly. "You really think we'd trust this idiot. We let him overhear us. He's just our calling card. He's become useless since the family reunion with precious Mommy." Her lip curls in disgust.

Wyck straightens, his hands fisting at his sides. Surprisingly, Griffin stiffens and moves closer to Wyck as though he can shield him from Lilah's taunt.

"I mean seriously, Griffin. Without your Wonder Twin power, what good are you?" She shrugs her blue-clad shoulder nonchalantly.

"What?" Wyck faces his brother. "Your Gift isn't working?"

Griffin shuffles from foot to foot before shaking his head.

"Wow, nothin' gets past you, huh?" She shakes her head. "Did you get those uncanny powers of perception from your dead mommy or your dead daddy?" Her animalistic smile gleams, and her eyes narrow.

Wyck's low growl rumbles in his chest, but Charlotte touches his face, drawing his attention. She shakes her head.

"Don't let her get to you," she says. "If you do, she wins."

"You *must* be the sister." Lilah puts her hands on her hips, her nostrils flaring. She looks her up and down. "Not much of an improvement." Lilah flicks her hair over her shoulder.

"It hasn't worked since, since... the cemetery," Griffin says.

Wyck blinks rapidly as though he can't process what Griffin has just admitted. "Why, Griff?"

"I don't—"Griffin begins.

"As touching as this brotherly bonding shit is, I don't have the time or the stomach for it." Lilah turns to Wyck and motions with a hand flick. "Go back to beating him. That's the first thing you've ever done I actually agree with."

"Why are you here?" Abby asks defiantly, her arms crossed over her chest and her head cocked.

Lilah saunters over to shimmer in front of Cooper, running her fingers up and down the center of her chest, before pointing to Abby. Without taking her eyes off Cooper, she purrs, "When you're dead, blondie and I are going to get acquainted. I know you like 'em short and fat," she says, this time talking to Cooper, "but I'll change all that."

Abby drops her arms and moves in front of Cooper, so close to Lilah that her image ripples before coming back into sharp focus.

Lilah laughs then sighs. "Whatever. I'm getting bored, so let's get this over with, shall we?"

"Absolutely," I reply, "I couldn't have said it better myself."

"Commander Matthews wants you to come willingly with him when he arrives," she states so matter-of-factly she could've been reciting her grocery list. She studies her nails, not bothering to look in my direction.

"Why doesn't he just come now, get it over already? And while we're on the subject, why didn't you follow Griffin in the flesh instead of this cowardly copy, Lilah? What are you waiting for?" My hand glows bright blue even though she's only a projection.

"Oh, don't you worry, Vivian. We'll all be here very soon. You'll be the first to know." She slithers closer until her image is so near I could touch her if she were real. "The commander wants you to see how reasonable he can be, and he says he'll be considerate of your sacrifice if you do. He'll save the others as his gift to you."

A prickle of fear shoots down my spine. From the corner of my eye I see my father move to stand in front of Charlotte. "What sacrifice?" I ask, but I already know I won't like the answer.

She stares casually at her nails, ignoring my question. "So what's your answer? Are you going to come willingly? Yes or no, Vivian?"

"What sacrifice, Lilah?" I repeat more forcefully, putting myself between her and the others.

"Answer first. Yes or no?" She finally deigns to look at me over her nails, her mouth a harsh slit in her face.

I glance back at the others, praying I'm not sealing someone's fate. "Tell him to go fuck himself, Lilah."

She smiles evilly as she drops her hand, suddenly very interested in our conversation. "I was hoping you'd say that." She shakes her head. "I've gotta give you credit, Vivian. You are ballsy—stupid, but ballsy." Taking a deep breath, she draws back her shoulders authoritatively.

"I've been instructed to leave a small reminder of Commander Matthews's power." She laces her fingers together and pushes them out in front of her, popping them as though she intends to do some serious work. "I've got a new trick courtesy of our generous leader, but unfortunately good for only one performance. So pay close attention, kiddos. Abracadabra," she murmurs then steps quickly to her left, around me.

Her hands move so fast I barely have time to register the movement before twin flashes of silver spring from her waistband into the air. The daggers slice lethally through the space between Wyck and her—two very real, very deadly blades.

"No!" I scream and fire a blast toward Lilah, but it zaps right through her. I move to shield Wyck, but I'm not in time to intercept the daggers.

Griffin leaps into action, turning his body so that he and Wyck are facing each other. His chest slams into Wyck's as the knives lodge deep into his back.

CHAPTER THIRTY-SIX

"GRIFFIN!" Wyck lowers his brother's limp body to the ground.

I round on Lilah, who looks at Griffin with shock before she huffs out a breath and crosses her arms.

"It's his fault. Never liked his dumb ass anyway! Oh well"—she shrugs—"one brother's as good as the next, and I've gotten rid of a pathetic loose end." Her eyes snap once more to mine. "Ta-ta, Vivian. I'll see *you* later." She finger waves, winks, and vanishes as quickly and soundlessly as she arrived.

We all converge on the brothers. Wyck is cradling Griffin's head against his chest, careful not to touch the knives' hilts where they protrude grotesquely from his back. Blood darkens Griffin's white t-shirt. His grisly gasp fills the silence, and when blood gurgles from his parted lips, an image of Aunt Charlotte's last moment flashes into my mind.

"I'm sorry, Griffin. I should have realized what was happening. I'm so sorry, brother." Tears trek down Wyck's face. Despite his earlier declaration of revenge, the reality is this boy in his arms is his twin, his constant companion since conception, and the pain he must be feeling is doubled by the knowledge that Griffin died for him. He willingly, knowingly stepped in the path of those knives to save Wyck.

Griffin's blood-coated smile is gruesome. His hand tightens on Wyck's shirt front. "Not your fault." He coughs, and more blood runs down the side of his face and drips onto the grass. "Whole thing, my fault."

"No, no, don't say that," Wyck pleads.

Griffin forces open his eyes when they slip closed. "Would not be here if not for me."

"You saved me. You're a hero." Wyck tries to smile. That's all Griffin ever wanted, to save the world, to use his Gift for something greater than himself. Ironically, it was his love for his brother, not his Gift at all, that made him into what he dreamed of being.

Griffin's eyes flash with gratitude, his mouth parted on the semblance of a final smile before he goes completely still, and his hand slips down the front of Wyck's shirt to land limply on the ground beside him.

Easton kneels and slides Griffin's eyelids closed. Wyck looks unseeing into Easton's eyes, but when Easton moves to take Griffin's body from Wyck, he clutches his brother forcefully against him. Griffin's white-blond hair is pink with his blood.

"No! No!" he yells, his arms and hands coated with Griffin's blood. "You can't take him from me! He's all I have left! You can't have him!"

Charlotte's touch on Wyck's shoulder draws his attention. "You have to let him go, Wyck. He's gone."

He shakes his head as a tear spills from his shiny eyes. "He saved me. He's my brother."

I kneel in front of him, next to Easton. "She's right. Let Easton take him."

Even though he's looking right at me, I don't think it's me he's seeing, and for a second, I think he hasn't registered what I've said. But then he gently lowers Griffin's body into Easton's arms. Easton adjusts Griffin's weight and clambers awkwardly to his feet. Harrison moves quickly to help, and the two of them walk away toward the other side of the house.

Wyck's lost expression breaks my heart as he allows Charlotte to help him stand. He's suffered so much, and I'm glad he has her to help him through this. Charlotte's gentleness is exactly what Wyck needs.

I'm still kneeling next to the grass stained red with the blood of my one-time friend when Wyck's eyes go to mine.

"Promise me, Princess," he says, forcefully.

I know exactly what he wants, have felt that same thing more times than I can count. He and Griffin may have been at odds when Griffin died, but they were still brothers, and Griffin made a selfless sacrifice to save him. He wants reassurance that we will avenge his brother.

"I promise, Wyck. Whatever it takes." My voice shakes with unreleased anger and my need for revenge.

"When they come, she's all mine." He turns toward Charlotte again and takes her hand as she leads him to the house.

*   *   *

An hour later my father is pouring steaming coffee into Charlotte's mug. After convincing Wyck to shower, she returned to the tense group gathered around the kitchen table.

"Where did you put him?" she asks, reaching down to rub Petey's head after spooning honey into her mug.

Harrison replaces the coffee pot and motions out the window toward a small shed at the edge of the yard. "We wrapped him in a canvas tarp and laid him in the storage building for now until Wyck can tell us what he wants to do."

"Will we have to report it to authorities?" Cooper asks, readjusting his long legs under the table.

"We *should*. But I'm not sure that's the best thing," Harrison is leaning against the counter. "There will be a lot of questions that I'm not certain how we'll answer."

"I can't believe that bitch killed Griffin." Abby shakes her head and takes a sip of her coffee.

"You heard her, sunshine. She was tryin' to kill Wyck." Cooper reaches out for her hand.

"But why? What was the point of it?" Abby asks.

"Power, it's always about power." Harrison turns to look once again out the window toward the storage shed.

"But if he's so strong, why didn't he try to hurt us all?" Charlotte asks.

"He'd be giving up his leverage." Easton stretches out and leans back in his chair.

I nod. "It's a way to keep me in line, Charlotte." Her brows draw together. "He can't kill these three"—I motion to Easton, Abby, and Cooper—"because he knows that will accomplish exactly the opposite reaction. He needs them alive to force me to do what he wants. He'd never hurt you because of his brother." Harrison turns and locks eyes with me before sighing and turning to Charlotte.

"She's right, honey. He wouldn't hurt either of us, so that leaves—"

"Me... and Griffin," Wyck says desolately from the doorway where his wet hair is dripping onto his t-shirt. She hurries to him, hugging him tightly. For a minute, he rests his head on her shoulder, her tiny body seemingly supporting his. "Griffin was Hoyt's biggest supporter until a few weeks ago, so Lilah was probably told to go after me, not Griffin. Griffin was the distraction. She couldn't have guessed he'd step in the path of those daggers."

"So what do we do now?" Cooper stands and stretches his arms over his head. "Do we just wait for him again?"

"You should go, you and Abby," Easton says. "Vivian was right when she said it was time for you two to go."

"Yeah." I nod. Abby starts to argue, but I put up my hand. "We talked about this, Ab. You have to go tonight."

"But what if he's waiting for them?" Charlotte asks.

We all exchange looks, the reality of her question dawning on each of us. "She's right."

"He's probably watching us, like, right now!" Abby exclaims, glancing around as though she'll find him hiding behind the fridge.

"I don't understand. If he won't attack me because of you, Dad, why does he go after Vivian? She's your daughter, too."

"Because he doesn't see it that way. I'm not so much Harrison's daughter as I am our mother's power. I'm not a person in his eyes, just a weapon." I shrug. And although my father's brow wrinkles like the knowledge pains him, he doesn't bother to deny it. Charlotte's mouth drops open, and her eyes widen.

"Vivian, I don't... I'm sorry. I didn't realize," she says, leaving Wyck's side to wrap one arm around me. I smile despite the seriousness of the situation. She really is so good. She reminds me more and more of her namesake.

"It's okay, Charlotte. *He* might think that, but *I* don't."

"Neither do the rest of us, honey." Harrison crosses his arms over his chest. "He's scared, Vivian. I know my brother, and you scare him because you're uncontrollable. He won't stop. His fear of you won't let him. If he can't control you…" He stops and shakes his head.

"I'm not afraid, not anymore, and when he comes—"

"We'll be ready," Wyck says, his navy eyes afire with the need for vengeance.

I glance around at everyone, and one at a time, they all nod their agreement. I just hope none of the rest of us shares Griffin's fate.

CHAPTER THIRTY-SEVEN

"ARE YOU SURE ABOUT THIS? It isn't too late to change your mind," I ask as Wyck stares down at the deep hole at his feet.

"No, it needs to be this way. We can't do this the normal way." He hasn't taken his eyes from the yawning hole.

"Do you at least want to wait till morning?" Charlotte asks.

Easton hands the shovel to Cooper and wipes his dirt-covered hands on his jeans. He and Cooper have taken turns digging for the last hour. After laying it aside, Cooper reaches out his hand and helps Easton climb from the hole.

Wyck glances around at the setting sun peeking through the trees. "No, I don't want to wait. We need to do this before nightfall so we can get back inside." He looks over at Harrison. "Thank you for letting me do this here. It's really peaceful. Despite what he became in the end, Griffin deserves peace." He shifts his gaze downward and brushes at his eyes.

The lump that's taken up temporary residence in my throat tightens until finally I'm wiping at my own eyes. Taking a shuddering breath, Wyck lifts his gaze and nods to Easton. Easton and Cooper walk a few feet away and retrieve Griffin's canvas-covered body from behind us, where we've all been studiously ignoring it. Using rope, they respectfully lower it into the chasm. Charlotte steps away from Wyck's side, but he reaches for her hand and pulls her back to him.

"You want to say somethin' before we..." Cooper motions toward the discarded dirt mound piled high next to the grave.

Wyck clears his throat. "I'm sorry it ended this way, Griffin. I love you." His words are barely audible as he bends to pick up a handful of dirt and toss it on top of the canvas then he begins walking back through the trees toward the house, pulling Charlotte behind him.

I grab Easton's hand, feeling the dirt still on his palm. Petey affectionately nuzzles his head against my other hand like he needs comforting, too, and we watch in silence as Cooper fills the hole.

"What do we do now?" Abby asks, peering over her glasses at me. "We wait."

*   *   *

Night passes quietly, too quietly. All of us are on edge waiting for the next assault. Easton and I fell asleep on the couch watching late-night talk shows until I awoke with a start hours later. Someone, my father I'm guessing, had turned off the television and covered us both with blankets. After that, sleep was as far away as my peace of mind, and I stared out into the darkness until dawn pinkened the sky then exchanged my cami and yoga pants for a ratty t-shirt and jeans. If today's the day I face Hoyt, at least I'll be comfortable if not well-rested.

When a groggy Charlotte emerges from her room with Petey bounding next to her, I'm in the kitchen pouring water into the coffee pot.

"Come on," she says, motioning him to the back door. He shoots like a bullet from the porch and into the yard.

I watch him for a second out the window, sniffing along the ground searching for that perfect doggy spot to do his business before I retrieve two mugs from the cabinet. When I turn back, he's running full speed across the yard toward the woods, probably chasing a squirrel. Must be nice to be a dog.

"Thanks for making coffee," Charlotte says, distracting me from my thoughts of Petey.

"You're welcome. I've been up for a while, so I figured I might as well." I fill our mugs and hand hers over.

She yawns while spooning in honey. "So I'm not the only one who couldn't sleep last night," she says. "If I'd known you were up, too, we could've kept each other company."

"I think I would have liked that." And I actually mean it. I would have enjoyed spending time with my sister. She smiles before sipping her coffee.

"Got a cup of that for your old dad?" Harrison asks, stumbling into the kitchen in his rumpled white t-shirt and black sweats. He stretches his arms over his head.

"Sure." Charlotte fills another mug.

He plops down tiredly at the table and scrubs his hand over his face and into his hair. His green eyes go to mine, and he smiles tenderly. "Come sit next to me," he says, patting the cushioned bench. Charlotte sets the mug in front of him before she sits down on his right. As I walk toward them, he kisses her cheek and squeezes her before thanking her for the coffee.

How weird is this—me, sitting with my father and my sister, at a table that reminds me of my aunt's kitchen, in a house that is now my home, waiting for my uncle to come kill me? Pretty screwed up even for me.

"Isn't this nice, the three of us, my girls and me?" Harrison smiles broadly, green eyes twinkling. He pulls us into a sideways bear hug.

"That's just what I was thinking," I reply with something close to a smile.

Charlotte reaches across the table and touches my hand. "I'm really glad you're here, Vivian."

"Yeah, me too." I nod. I am glad. I think. This whole sister-father relationship is still so strange to me. I want to get to know them both, but it's going to take some time to feel like it's normal.

"I'll go feed Petey." I need to escape this closeness for now. When I jump up from the table, Harrison grimaces slightly but nods his acceptance. He obviously realizes I'm not quite ready for a family portrait moment. Dashing to the back porch a little too quickly to be nonchalant, I pull on my shoes and grab and fill Petey's dish before rushing outside into the fresh, morning air. I set the bowl down on the steps as Charlotte had done and call Petey's name loudly.

The porch door squeaks in protest as Charlotte steps out behind me. "Are you okay? You took off so fast, I was afraid you might be upset."

I shake my head. "I'm fine. Just needed some air." I hope she understands, but I'm not ready to go into my feelings with her yet. She nods and smiles reassuringly. Her pink pajamas and little-girl braids make her look so young and innocent. It's hard to believe we're the same age.

That's when I feel it, a tingle in my chest. An awareness that causes me to stiffen creeps along my skin, prickling my arms and legs. I reach out with my mind, and there's the slightest something's-not-right sensation nibbling at the edges.

"Petey?" I call again, starting down the steps. When I get no slobbering run across the yard, I start for the woods. I don't want to alarm Charlotte or put her in danger, but my senses are going into overdrive. Something—better yet, someone—is in those woods. "I'll go look for Petey, okay?" I attempt a reassuring expression, but she's not buying it. Her eyes narrow.

"I'll go with you," she says, starting down the steps as well.

"No!" I exclaim. "That is, uh, I'd like to take a walk alone."

She quirks a brow and crosses her arms over her chest but stays put as I walk toward the woods. I keep calling until I reach the trees. It's eerily silent, no birds, no scurrying little animals, just my breathing and my crunching footsteps. Energy spikes through my body, and I tense in preparation for a threat I can't yet see.

A strange smell raises goose bumps along my skin. It's acrid and almost stinging, smoky and unpleasant but somehow familiar. As I get deeper into the forest, the smell becomes stronger, and my stomach twists as I realize what it is. Burnt hair.

"What's that smell?" Charlotte is suddenly right next to me, clutching my arm, her eyes as wide as saucers.

"Charlotte! I told you to stay put!" I whisper-yell. How did I not sense her behind me? Some great protector I am!

"Yeah, well, I didn't. So what's that smell? Smells like when I leave the flattening iron in my hair too long."

"Charlotte, go back to the house and get Harrison and Wyck." The trees are still, waiting.

"No, I'm not leaving," she says with the petulance of a six-year-old. "Remind you of anybody?" She puts her hand on her hip and quirks her lips.

Shaking my head, I glance to my right, and I see a blackened lump that stands out unnaturally on the forest floor. Gray-white wisps of smoke rise from it. I creep cautiously closer, and I realize the 'it' is Petey.

"Is that—" Charlotte gasps and starts forward, but I pull her behind me.

Petey's lying in a circle of charred ground about twenty feet away. I run toward him with Charlotte on my heels. His entire body is shaking, almost convulsing. His eyes are still open, and when I kneel beside him he whimpers and tries to press his nose into my leg. His hair is a melted mass of black against his bleeding skin.

"Oh, Petey," I whisper, touching his muzzle gently, "I'm so sorry, boy." I want so badly to hold him, but his pain would be too intense. It's inconceivable that he's even still alive. This is Zeb's work.

Charlotte gasps and drops to her knees, her hands over her open mouth. "Petey?" Tears spill from her storm-gray eyes and over her hands. "Petey," she sobs, reaching to touch him. When he tries to move closer to her and whines loudly, she draws her hand back and covers both her eyes. I press her face into my shoulder while peering all around us. The threat is there; I can feel it. I have to get Charlotte to the house, to safety.

"We have to go back—now." I stand and try to pull her to her feet.

Her bewildered eyes drop to Petey. "They did this, didn't they? Why, Vivian? Why would they hurt my dog?"

"Charlotte, Lilah tried to kill Wyck and succeeded in killing Griffin, remember?" I gently urge her to her feet, but her eyes stay transfixed on Petey. She nods, but I don't think she truly understands my words or her actions. Grabbing her hand, I tug her forward, but she won't budge and yanks her hand from mine.

"We can't leave him. He needs help. We have to get him to the vet." She refuses to see that Petey is beyond help now. The greatest help we could give him would be to end his pain.

"Charlotte"—I sigh, knowing we don't have time for gentleness. "Petey's dying. We could too if we don't hurry. Let's go." I pull her more firmly this time, but again she stands her ground.

"No! I won't leave him! He's in pain!"

Gritting my teeth and trying to remain calm, I glance down at Petey, his eyes glazed with agony. As long as he lives, she won't leave, and I can't leave her. I have to finish him, and when our eyes meet again, she knows my thoughts without hearing them. Her chin trembles, the tears flowing without stopping over already-wet cheeks.

Kneeling again, she touches his muzzle as I had a few minutes ago before leaning in to kiss the spot. "I love you, boy," she whispers.

She stands and nods without looking at me then turns her back to Petey, unable to watch as I kneel and place my hand upon his body.

"I'm sorry, Petey." My hand glows blue for only a second, and Petey's eyes close peacefully.

"We'll come back for his body as soon as we can," I say, trying to assure her but not really knowing if we will or not. She needs to hear it all the same. She nods and wipes her face with the back of her hand.

"Let's go." She doesn't resist this time, but as we turn in the direction of the house, the hair along my nape stands. Charlotte inhales sharply and holds her breath. She senses something, too.

"Do you feel that? They're watching us," Charlotte whispers in a rush of air. Her breathing tells me she's on the verge of all out panic. She grabs my right hand but quickly releases it when I unintentionally give her a shock.

I have to get her back. The only way I know to do that is to shield us both, run like hell, and hope they don't follow until I can warn the others. It's possible that I could shield her from a distance while she escaped for reinforcements and I stay behind to draw their fire, but I know my power will be stronger if we stay together. I've never really shielded anyone without close proximity, and I can't take the chance now. Plus, I'm guessing Hoyt has plenty of backup, definitely Zeb judging by Petey and probably Lilah and Ferguson. Maybe more if he's had time to bring in new recruits.

"Okay, Charlotte, you have to listen and do as I tell you. We're gonna hold hands and run back to the house. I'll shield us in an energy field, but don't stop running no matter what you see," I add, thinking of Lilah's illusions, "not even if it looks like the forest disappears. Keep running. Understand?" I whisper, so close our noses nearly touch.

"That's our plan? Run?" she asks, her face growing even more desperate.

"You got a better one? Any tricks you haven't shown me?" I know it's a shitty plan, but I'm doing the best I can here. Not like her *Back to the Future* Gift does us much good right now.

She shakes her head so forcefully that her braids whack her cheeks. "No, no, you're right—hold hands and run." She starts to grab my right hand again, thinks better of it, and reaches across for my left.

"Ready?" She nods. Closing my eyes, I imagine the iridescent orb surrounding us, and when I open them, she's reaching out in awe to touch the inside surface. It ripples and crackles, full of static charge. The energy isn't a warm and fuzzy kind. It's strong, but it will have to be to protect us both. I squeeze her hand, and we take off.

CHAPTER THIRTY-EIGHT

Fear

She has seen.
She will go to him.
She will join with him.
She will tell him all.
She will show him,
in his mind the evil
that I have done,
that I have become.
She will convince him
not to forgive me.
She will convince him
not to return to me.
She will shine
as her mother did,
and he will be lost to me
forever.
She has won.

CHAPTER THIRTY-NINE

THE SHIELD MUFFLES every sound except Charlotte's labored breathing behind me. I'm practically dragging her over the uneven forest floor littered with twigs, branches, and roots of all sizes, and because I'm focusing so intensely on the orb, my emotions get the better of me. The sunlight weakens, and the clouds move in.

The rain plops at first in fat drops on the orb's surface before becoming a steady, pounding rhythm. While we're protected inside, the ground outside of our immediate area is not, and soon Charlotte's slipper-clad feet slip over the slick surface.

The first time she stumbles, I jerk her up before she actually touches the ground, but the second time, we aren't so lucky. Her pink slipper sticks in the curve of a tree root while her other foot slips, and she slaps the ground hard, sprawling face-first at the foot of a giant oak. Her fingers slide from my hold and so does my focus. The shield immediately vanishes.

As I'm reaching out to pull her up, Ferguson, wearing his black uniform and loaded with weapons, steps out from a tree about ten feet behind us. At the expression on my face, Charlotte turns and spots him over her shoulder. He smiles triumphantly, oblivious to the rain slashing against his face as he lifts the patch over his right eye.

The earth begins to shake, raining leaves and loose twigs down around us. I grab frantically for her, but the shaking intensifies until I can no longer stand.

The root seems to grow before my eyes as the dirt all around it dances and shakes away. I fall to my knees, crawling toward her, but more roots pop from the ground. It looks like the enormous trees are reaching out for support. A dead, wind-twisted limb breaks loose high above me, and I watch as it crashes down toward me. I'm forced to crab-scurry backward on my butt, separating us even further and giving Ferguson the chance he needs. He yanks the patch back into place and lunges forward.

"Vivian!" She screams as he rushes up behind her and wraps his arms around her upper body and waist. He pins her arms to her sides as he lifts her off the ground enough to keep her feet from touching. When she kicks viciously, he slides one arm up and around her throat, tightening his hold until she gasps and stops kicking. Her face turns pink then red.

"Stop it, Ferguson! You'll kill her!" I yell, jumping to my feet now that the shaking has stopped.

He laughs and glances up, rolling his eyes. "And why would I do that? I just got her. We haven't had time to get to know each other yet."

He smirks and rubs his cheek against her hair, inhaling deeply. "So, sweet." He sneers in satisfaction. "You can blame yourself for this. If you hadn't turned on the waterworks, she wouldn't have slipped, and I wouldn't have captured her. You made this so much easier, Vivian. Thank you." He starts backward, grinning. "Stay put. Wouldn't want me to slip trying to get away and break her neck, now would you?" he asks, dragging Charlotte deeper into the forest again.

Before I can rush forward after her, the weak daylight begins to vanish. The trees and sky fade slowly to black, the light draining away. Darkness claws at me, pressing close like a blanket. Damp air invades my lungs. Something scurries near my leg. It crawls up my arm and into my hair, clicking close to my ear. I scream and bat it away. Hundreds of tiny bodies swarm my arms, legs, and hair. I can't keep up. I open my mouth to scream but the teeming mass surges toward my face.

Lilah. She's working her Gift, and though my brain tells me it's not real, my body goes into panic mode. I'm breathing so rapidly I begin to hyperventilate. I fall back on my butt, opening my palm to produce a light source, but I'm so upset, nothing happens, which terrifies me even more until all rational thought flees in the face of it.

I pull my legs up, wrap my arms around them, and drop my head onto my knees. I try to slow my breathing. But the creatures mass on my exposed skin. I squeeze my eyes tight. "This isn't real. This isn't real. This isn't real," I whisper over and over. Something grasps my shoulder, and I scream loudly.

"Vivian! It's me!" My eyes fly open at Easton's voice. The darkness is gone, but the rain is still sheeting down, soaking his jeans. He pulls me up against his bare chest, but I can't seem to get close enough.

"Get them off of me, Easton!" I scream, swatting at rain drops but still feeling the insects. I tromp on his bare feet until he finally slings me into his arms.

"There's nothing there!" He squeezes me tightly against him. "You're hallucinating!" he yells over the rain's fury, but I continue to scrub my arms and hair, trying to wipe away the sensation.

"Where's Charlotte?" From beside Easton, my father takes my face between his hands, forcing my eyes to focus on him instead of the imaginary insects. The rain darkens his hair and plasters his shirt to his chest.

My trembling becomes so severe I can no longer speak or even think clearly. I look in the direction Ferguson dragged her. Harrison runs past Easton into the forest.

"We have to get you inside!" He jogs the rest of the way out of the trees, through the backyard, and doesn't stop until we are inside the house.

Abby rushes toward us, but Easton moves past her, Cooper, and Wyck where they stand in the kitchen. When we reach the bathroom, he closes the door, sits me down on the toilet lid, and removes my wet shirt, shoes, and jeans before wrapping me in two towels. Kneeling in front of me, he briskly rubs my arms, legs, and back until I finally stop shaking.

"What happened out there, babe? Where's Charlotte?" He grabs another towel for my hair.

At the mention of her name, my heart rate leaps. "Charlotte! Oh, Easton, I left her! I have to go back!" I jump up, dislodging the towels, but he pushes me back onto the seat.

"You can't go back right now. You're a wreck. What happened to you?" He assesses my arms and legs with his hands, his eyes the color of a stormy sea.

"Ferguson took her! They have Charlotte!" They've taken another Charlotte from me. My throat tightens as panic begins to rise. Not again. I can't let them kill her like they did my aunt. I won't!

"They can't have her! I have to go!" I succeed in jumping up, but he blocks my path, wrapping his arms around me, pinning my right hand to my side.

"No! You aren't going back out there right now! Calm down!" I struggle against him, pushing him with my free left hand, but it's no use. Without my Gift, he's physically too strong, and I'm too rattled to brainjack him into releasing me.

"You don't understand! Ferguson has her! They set Petey on fire! You have to let go!" I'm yelling, but it only takes a half a minute to turn to sobs against his chest. "They have her. They took her, and I didn't stop them."

"Vivian"—my father's unbelievably calm voice calls from right outside the door—"I need you to open the door and tell us what happened."

His lack of alarm only increases my shame. I failed him because I failed her, yet his tone is as steady as ever. He can't possibly realize the danger she's in if he can stand there calmly asking me to open the door as if he's asking me what I'd like for lunch.

Easton peers down at me, his brows raised in silent question. When I nod, he releases me and moves toward the door. I sink again to the only seat in the room, clutching my towels around me. The towels remind of my first meeting with my father. What a mess I've made of his and Charlotte's lives! If not for me, Petey would be alive, and she'd be here with him.

Harrison's face is much less reassured than his voice. His brows are drawn sternly together. His mouth is set in a hard line, tension tightening his jaw, but he kneels, dripping on the bathroom floor and speaking to me like he's afraid I might break into jagged pieces.

"Honey, I need you to explain what happened," he says so quietly he's nearly whispering. Wyck, Abby, and Cooper, all three looking as though they rolled out of bed only minutes ago, crowd the doorway. I can't look at any of them. I drop my gaze to my hands twisted tightly in the towels. The quiet of the room is disturbed only by the pounding rain against the window.

"We... we were looking for... Petey." I take a deep breath which does absolutely nothing to make this any easier. How can I confess to him that I abandoned his daughter because of some imaginary bugs?

"He's... we found him." I chance a glance at my father. He nods.

"I found him, too." The understanding in his eyes releases a floodgate, and I begin to babble and shake my head.

"I should have forced her to turn back as soon as I realized she was there. I should never have walked over to him. How could I be so stupid? It was an obvious trap, and I let her walk right into it! I'm so sorry!" I look from him to Wyck, whose face is pale, his breathing heavy. "We were running back. I had us shielded but the rain! The damn rain!" I look toward the window. A sob escapes, and I bury my head in my hands like the coward I am.

"I couldn't control my emotions, and the rain made the ground slick. When she fell—" I draw a shuddering breath, remembering the terrified expression on her face as she realized Ferguson was behind us. Harrison pulls my hands from my face and grips them in his own. "I lost concentration and dropped the shield for just a second. Ferguson was waiting."

He nods, motioning around with his hand. "We felt the quake, but we couldn't move until it stopped." For the first time I notice the cracks in the walls, the shampoo bottles lying on the floor.

"That's how we knew," Easton says, water still dripping from his black hair onto his forehead.

"He dragged her away, and I, I let him." I close my eyes.

"You didn't let him. He took her." Easton touches my head. "You were a wreck when we found you. Was it Lilah?"

I nod, not ready to relive that episode just yet. "I'll get her back. I promise."

My father shakes his head. "No, you won't. I will."

CHAPTER FORTY

SOMEONE TO FIGHT MY BATTLES, a champion. Isn't that what I've been wishing for? A knight in shining armor to take care of me, so I don't have to be afraid anymore? But I can't let him do this. I allowed this to happen, and I have to fix it, end it once and for all with my uncle.

"This is my fault, Harrison. I won't let you take the punishment for this. I'll go with him and do whatever he wants if he'll return Charlotte to you."

"No, you won't!" Easton shakes his head forcefully.

At the same time, Wyck says, "Me, too. We'll surrender together, Princess, and get her back in exchange."

"No! What the hell?" Easton yells, his face confused and his voice echoing forcefully against the tile. "Have you both lost your minds? It's not happening, so stop saying it! Stop thinking it!" He motions his hands in a 'so that's final' way.

"It's the easiest way to get her back." I look at Wyck. "We'll be fine as long as Hoyt doesn't figure out Charlotte has powers, too."

Wyck nods. "But how will we contact him?"

Easton steps between us, blocking our eye contact and turning to Wyck. "You think I'm gonna let either of you go to him willingly? What's the last six months been about if not to keep you two from him?"

"None of that matters anymore, Easton. He has Charlotte. Game over. He wins. I'm sick of this fight, and I won't see another person hurt because of some stupid Gift I never asked for!" A loud boom of thunder punctuates my frustration. I motion toward the window. "All of this, rain included, is my fault!"

"I should never have left him," Wyck mutters. "If I hadn't, Griffin would be alive, and I could be on the other side with them, keeping Charlotte safe."

"Well, that's a dumb comment!" Abby squints her glasses-free eyes at Wyck. "You wouldn't even have met her if not for Vivian." She flings her arm in my direction but keeps her eyes on Wyck. "You'd be one of *them*, you idiot! As for Griffin, he made his choice. He chose to fix a mess he helped screw up in the first place!" She points at us both. "Do you honestly think you sacrificing yourselves now is going to change anything? That's the cowards' way out, and I thought both of you had more guts than that!" She puts her hands on her hips.

Everyone stares silently at her in her cupcake-covered night pants and her Hello Kitty shirt, blonde curls poking in every direction at once.

"Well-said, Abby." Harrison nods his head slowly. "I couldn't have done better myself." He tenderly grips my knee. "You are most certainly not giving yourself up, and neither is Wyck. The last honorable act my brother did was help Charlotte and me escape. There's no way he's going to go quietly away again."

"Anyway, he's prob'ly already got a plan to keep all of ya'll," Cooper adds, leaning his big body against the door facing and pretty much forcing the others out of it.

"And I'll bet he knows about Charlotte's power, too. Otherwise, why bother kidnapping her? Why would he just leave you there and take her? He could have forced you to come with him in the forest or taken you while you were freakin' out. He obviously didn't want Charlotte when she was a baby, so why take her now?" Easton shakes his head thoughtfully. "No, he knows somehow, and he wants to force all of you to come with him. She's a bargaining chip for all three of you."

Harrison straightens, nods, and runs his hands through his wet hair. If this room were larger, he'd probably be pacing. "I agree. He's going to use her to force me back, too. Maybe he sensed her power when he projected Lilah to us, but at any rate, I think Easton's right."

"Yeah, well, that doesn't make me feel any better, *and* that makes you guys even more expendable!" I stand, too, keeping the towels firmly around me. "You'll just be collateral damage to him if we don't do something."

"We need a plan," Abby says. "How're we going to do it? Go in like outlaws with guns blazin'?" She holds up hands in the same way a little boy does when he's pretending to have a gun, "Or stealthy like ninjas?" She bends her knees in a fighting stance and chops the air.

"*You* don't need anything, except a closet to hide in." I cross my arms and nearly lose one of my towels.

"Uh, no way, weather girl!" she exclaims, snapping the fingers on one hand. "You do not get to give me that 'you have to stay safe' shit" — she glances sheepishly at my father — "this time. I'm helping. If you're forcing me to start back to high school without you, then I get to help!" She snaps again then crosses her arms.

My mouth drops open in shock. "Weather girl?" I look over at Easton, who's hiding a smile behind his hand and Cooper who isn't bothering to hide it at all.

She shrugs. "What else you wanna be called — static cling?" When Wyck snorts, she smiles, too. Soon, everyone is laughing, including me. Leave it to Abby to break the tension with her usual flare.

"I was thinkin' supreme ruler or goddess-on-high might be nice," I say, pinching her arm.

"More like you-must-be-high-if-you-think-I'm-calling-you-that." And with that parting shot, she marches her angry-cockatoo self out of the bathroom.

"Better just stick with Princess for now." Wyck yanks the corner of my towel and forces me to tighten my grip again before he follows Abby.

Cooper trails Wyck, slapping him on the back and muttering, "My sunshine's a spitfire, ain't she?"

When my father, Easton, and I are left alone, Harrison's face becomes serious again. "Get dressed, honey. We have to decide which it will be, cowboys or ninjas. Either way, I *will* have both my daughters back before nightfall." Then he, too, heads back down the hall.

Grabbing the towel ends and pulling me in close, Easton rests his chin on the top of my head. "This is it, isn't it? The end of it? I just have this feeling it's gonna be over today."

"I hope you're right, Easton." What if he's right but with a different kind of end? I pull back enough to look up at him. "If I don't survive this, promise you'll—"

"No." He shakes his head and releases me. "I won't listen to this. We've come too far; we're too close to it being over."

"But that's what I mean. If it's really the end—"

"No, Vivian! Don't you say it! We will have our happy ending!" He steps toward the door, refusing to look at me. "Now, listen to your dad and get dressed." He walks away without a glance back, but the anger in his voice sounds a lot like fear.

CHAPTER FORTY-ONE

"WOW, IT'S NEVER LIKE THIS IN THE MOVIES," Abby says with a sigh. Dressed all in black with her hair in a bun that's so tight she looks like her post-facelift mother, she flops down on the loveseat hard and nearly bounces me off of it.

The television is blaring theme music, but no one's really paying attention to it. Once we all decided our best option was to wait for Hoyt to contact us, Abby decided on the black getup, a cross between *Mission Impossible* and Starbuck's barista. I didn't have the heart to tell her how ridiculous she looked in that garb, but after her fifth flop in the past hour, I have to bite back my tart reply.

"What'd you expect, sunshine? In real life, the fire-throwin', scenery-changin', quakeman kidnapper doesn't throw a ransom note tied to a rock through the front window." Cooper shakes his head, and I'm not sure if he realizes how insane that sounds or if he's joking. Either way, it's true. "You gotta be patient."

"Yeah, like, not my strong suit." She huffs, getting up and heading into the kitchen again. When Abby's stressed, she falls back on her old coping mechanism, eating. She's eaten almost nonstop today. Every time she comes back from the kitchen she's holding something cheesy, sweet, or leftover in her hand.

"It better happen soon, or she's going to explode," Wyck says, rolling his eyes.

Cooper, Easton, and I both turn to give him the evil eye across the room where he's sitting on the floor, leaning against the cracked wall. When Charlotte does return she'll have plenty of repairs to keep her busy for a while.

"What?" he asks, throwing up his hands. "Am I lying? She's eaten all day!" He leans his head back and closes his eyes. "Sorry, I'm a dick for saying that. Don't tell her, okay?" he sighs.

"This waiting's got us all edgy." Harrison is preparing his pipe in the house before stepping out onto the front porch.

"Mind if I come with you?" I push up from the loveseat before he replies.

"Not at all." He half-smiles as though that's all he can manage at the moment, and holds open the door.

We both sit on the steps, the scene of our first real, father-daughter-spill-your-guts talk, and he lights the pipe, exhaling the sweet smoke that's usually so soothing. But all I can think about is poor Charlotte. My eyes tear, and Harrison puts his arm around me.

"It's going to be okay, honey. I promise," he says, kissing my forehead.

"Really, Harrison, how can you promise such a thing to the poor child?" Hoyt, in his black uniform, steps from the forest surrounding the house and strolls confidently toward the porch steps. On his heels are the others, Lilah, Zeb, and Ferguson, who's holding a handcuffed Charlotte by the upper arm.

Harrison and I stand in unison. He drops his pipe to the ground.

"You still have that disgusting pipe?" Hoyt shakes his head and tsks. "I never understood that habit of yours."

Harrison snorts in anger. "And I never understood your need to control everyone around you."

Hoyt smiles. "Touché, brother." He turns his black eyes to me. "Vivian, my dear, you are becoming quite the nuisance. I'm afraid my patience is wearing thin." He moves closer, his glassy, dead eyes shining even though the sky is still cloudy. "Lilah informed me of the unfortunate accident with Griffin." He shakes his head in mock regret. "I had hoped to redeem Griffin after reconditioning his brother, of course." He flips his hand and tosses his head nonchalantly at Griffin's sacrifice. "C'est la vie."

Harrison breathes heavily beside me, his chest heaving with suppressed anger. "Charlotte, are you okay?"

She opens her mouth to answer, but Ferguson yanks her arm hard. When she winces, Harrison starts forward. Thunder growls overhead and the sky darkens. I glance up. I'm not responsible for this one, so either a real storm is rolling in, or my father is losing his control.

Hoyt wags his finger and shakes his head. "Uh, uh, brother, you stay there. You see, I had intended to keep you and darling Charlotte"—he smirks at me when he says her name, no doubt to remind me of Aunt Charlotte's fate—"but imagine my surprise at discovering her little secret." His eyes narrow as he clenches his teeth. "You lied to me, Harrison. She's Gifted."

My father shakes his head, his lips tight. "I never lied to you. I didn't know about her Gift for many years, but I wouldn't have told you anyway. You destroyed our lives when you killed Violet." Thunder peels, and Wyck appears in the shadowy doorway. His hand is turning the knob, but I give the tiniest shake of my head. He needs to stay hidden for as long as possible. We need the element of surprise. He reluctantly releases it, and I hear his voice in my mind.

I'm coming out the back door, Princess.

Before I can tell him to wait for my signal, Hoyt motions Ferguson forward so that Charlotte is within reach then flicks his wrist backward. Ferguson grimaces at no longer being the center of attention and moves to stand next to Lilah and Zeb.

"I gave you your life and that of Charlotte. You owed me. You should have told me after my generosity." He strokes Charlotte's blonde braid.

"Generosity? That's what you call it? You killed the woman I love! You nearly killed Vivian! I hate you!" He flings up his hand and the waiting clouds erupt, emptying in a gush. But before the rain reaches the ground, it swirls into a spiral of water, a whirlpool in the air. When Harrison spins his hand, it heads straight for Hoyt.

Surprise flickers across Hoyt's face before he too raises his hand. The swirling water veers sharply left, toward Ferguson, Lilah, and Zeb. The three slam back on the ground, and the water falls harmlessly, drenching them.

Hoyt's chest heaves, his face twisted with fury, before he takes a deep breath and closes his eyes. When he opens them he again wears his mask of control. "Brother, that was unwise. What if you'd hit my precious niece?" He tugs her hair hard, forcing her to her knees. She cries out. "I'm somewhat surprised that you can still use your Gift," he says calmly before pulling a knife from a holster at his hip. The tip flashes as he adjusts his hold on Charlotte's hair, pulling her head back and exposing her throat.

"Daddy!" she screams, terror making her voice high and unnatural, as he presses the blade to her skin.

"Hoyt, stop! I'll do whatever you want! Just don't hurt her!" Harrison holds up his hands in surrender.

"But only seconds ago you were willing to risk her life to kill me? Have you changed your mind?" He smiles evilly. "Shall we play a game? Tell you what. I'll let you kill me, but I take her with me. What do you say, brother? You and Vivian will be free and safe. But poor, little Charlotte" — he shakes his head in mock regret — "well, she'll be dead. How badly do you want to save your other daughter, the one you abandoned all those years ago?"

He faces me. "It would seem he owes us both, my dear." Hoyt glances up thoughtfully. "Perhaps, I should let Vivian decide. She will most assuredly have a different perspective, will she not?"

"Hoyt, I know you believe I've betrayed you by not telling —"

"No, brother!" Hoyt whips back to Harrison. "You betrayed me long before that! When you chose that woman over me, you betrayed me! When you begged for my help in making you and" — he presses the blade harder, and a trickle of blood flows down the smooth curve of Charlotte's neck — "this creature disappear! You chose life without me to save the byproduct of an experiment, Harrison! She wasn't even supposed to exist, and you chose her!"

He's losing it, and he's going to kill Charlotte in the process.

"If you were going to choose, you should have at least chosen the powerful one! It's incomprehensible that you would pick a useless girl over your own brother!"

From the corner of my eye I catch movement at the side of the house — Wyck. Ferguson, Lilah, and Zeb struggle drunkenly to their feet. I have to distract Hoyt until Wyck can do whatever the hell he's going to do.

"She's not useless, Uncle." With a confidence that's as fake as Lilah's blue-streaked hair, I step off the porch and past my father.

Charlotte's seeking gaze nearly ruins my artificial composure. Hoyt pulls back his shoulders but only slightly relieves the pressure of his blade against Charlotte's neck.

"I already know she's a Twister, so your attempts at distracting me from my purpose are in vain," he says with a sneer, but he's more interested than he pretends to be.

"Yeah, you know she's a Twister, but have you seen her use it?" When he raises one brow, I know I have him. "Oh, the great Commander Matthews hasn't bothered to investigate this never-be-fore-seen Gift?"

"Why do I need to? She confessed, quite easily by the way, nothing like the torture I would have had to force upon you had the roles been reversed." Something akin to pride crosses his face. "She sees the past and allows others to see it. I'd like to keep her, but if it must be this way..." he shrugs.

Good, he's made the same mistake I did, underestimating the power of seeing the past, of seeing *his* past. I snort. "You really should experience it first before you eliminate her Gift for eternity, oh wise one." I lock eyes with my sister. I want badly to speak into her mind, but with Hoyt so close, that's impossible. I need her to remind him of his love for his brother. It's our only shot out of this without a total bloodbath. "After all, you've already lost Griffin and most likely his twin." I squint hard at Charlotte, hoping she understands. When her eyes light up and she nods almost imperceptibly, I know she gets my drift. We need to show Hoyt how much he loved his brother. I only hope she's able to pull up a good memory.

"Fine, but you join us, my dear, while the others stay behind. This cooperation from you leaves a bad taste. Do not make me regret my decision or she will pay the penalty." He doesn't sheath his knife, but he does pull Charlotte to her feet.

"No tricks from me. I only want to show you that my sister could be useful." I reach out for her hand, but Hoyt jerks her back. "We all have to touch if I'm going to join you." He allows me to hold her hand, and I squeeze it tightly and nod encouragingly at her.

"It will help if you close your eyes until we're in your past," she says quietly, her voice strained. "Think of a memory from child-hood, something happy will be easier."

He raises one eyebrow and stares at her so long I'm certain he's changed his mind. At last, he motions the others forward. "Bind his hands securely, Ferguson, and hold him away from the house where I assume the others are plotting some daring but failed rescue attempt." Then he sighs loudly, returns the knife to the case, and closes his eyes. "Fail to peak my interest, niece, and you will sorely regret it."

Charlotte wastes no time, and immediately we are transported back.

CHAPTER FORTY-TWO

A LAKE SHIMMERS IN THE SUN. The grass is so green it doesn't look real. Two young, blond boys with eyes just as green are racing toward the water, stripping off their shirts and shoes before diving from the bank into the water. When they surge to the surface, they laugh and splash each other.

"I beat you this time!" yells the one missing his front teeth.

"I let you win 'cause you cry like a baby if I don't!" laughs the other as he swims in the opposite direction. "But I won't let you this time!"

I chance a glance at Hoyt. His forehead wrinkles like he's is trying to make sense of what he's seeing. When I look back at the lake, the boys are splashing each other again.

"Hoyt, watch this," says the toothless one, as he twirls his index finger in water. A miniature whirlpool spins slowly at first then gains speed until the other's eyes grow large with wonder.

"When did you figure out you could do that?" asks Hoyt.

My father shrugs. "When you were studying yesterday." His nose wrinkles in disgust. "Why do you study all the time? It's summer! We have a break!"

Hoyt, his face smooth and still innocent, smiles. "I like it. It makes me smart, and if I get smarter, someday we'll go all over the world together."

"Where? Where will go?"

"Anywhere you wanna go, that's where. We won't be stuck here all the time. We'll see stuff and do stuff! I'll take care of you." He smiles and puts his arm around his twin.

"But what if I get lost?" Harrison asks, eyes wide with little-boy fear.

"Then I will find you," Hoyt says as confidently. "Always, brother."

"But I don't wanna go anywhere. Except here, our lake." He grins and stops circling his finger in the water. Hoyt grins back, and with a flick of his own index finger, he sends the whirlpool sailing into the center of the lake where it gradually stops spinning and ripples to nothing.

I find myself smiling at the two as they dunk each other until they're both sputtering but still laughing. Hard to imagine that they could ever become bitter enemies. Charlotte squeezes my hand and motions with her chin toward Hoyt. A tear streaks unheeded down his cheek.

When he notices us watching, he swipes it with the back of his hand as his mouth tightens. He grabs Charlotte's arm. "Let's go," he says through gritted teeth.

When next I blink, we've returned to the front yard. Ferguson, Lilah, and Zeb surround Harrison. I reach out for Wyck, praying that Hoyt is still lost in the past and can't sense my mental feelers. He's there, at the corner of the house.

"Well, my dear, I don't often admit I'm wrong—perhaps because I am usually not—but you may have been correct. Her Gift could prove useful after all." He pushes Charlotte away from him and into Ferguson's arms. "It would seem we are keeping this one, Ferguson. You're in charge of her acclimation."

Ferguson's mouth quirks lewdly at one corner. "My pleasure, Commander Matthews." Lilah's eyes narrow.

"Why are we keeping her?" Lilah whines. "Isn't one enough trouble?" She glares over at me.

"Lilah, we are keeping her, and if you complain any more we will have another opening on our little squad. Secure her." He motions with his fingers like he's shooing away a fly.

Ferguson grabs Charlotte's wrists in one hand and pulls handcuffs from his uniform pocket.

"Let me help." Lilah yanks Charlotte's hand. When Charlotte lets out a yelp, Wyck makes his move.

Stepping from the corner of the house, he yells, "Stop!"

Everyone stills mid-motion except for Charlotte and me as he runs forward and pulls her hands from Lilah's. I search Ferguson for the key to Harrison's restraints. When I find it I open my father's handcuffs.

"Go to the house," he says, not looking at her but instead yanking a set of familiar daggers from the waistband of his jeans.

"No, I won't leave you two and Dad!" She shakes her head.

"Charlotte, go! I don't want you to see—"

Before he can finish, the others begin to move. Lilah's smirk vanishes when she realizes it's Wyck, not Charlotte, standing before her.

"Remember these?" he asks, holding the daggers close to her face. Without another word he plunges them into her chest. Lilah gasps and grabs at the knives. It only takes an instant before she collapses, her glassy-eyed stare to the sky.

"Wyck, take her and go!" I yell.

Before he can move, Ferguson bellows loudly and tackles Wyck to the ground almost on top of Lilah's body. In a reverse replay of the cemetery, Ferguson wails on Wyck. When I run forward, Zeb steps into my path.

"Kid, we aren't enemies. It's not your fight. Move aside."

"I can't," he says, producing a fire ball in his hand. "He'll kill me if I don't fight."

"Guess we're gonna do this the hard way again."

"I'll take care of this." My father steps beside me. Zeb's eyes widen. I'm guessing he's remembering his impromptu shower.

Charlotte pounds and yanks on Ferguson, but he has his hands wrapped securely around Wyck's throat. Wyck claws at them, but his face is turning purple.

The front door slams and Easton, Cooper, and Abby are running toward us.

"Charlotte move!" I yell, but she's so focused she doesn't hear me. "Easton, grab her!" He grabs her around the waist, and I blast out an energy orb. It slams into the side of Ferguson's body and flings him away from Wyck.

Charlotte rushes over, pressing her fingers against the artery in Wyck's neck. We all hold our breaths until she nods to us.

"Get him inside!" Cooper tosses Wyck over his shoulder. "Easton, go with them they might need you!" He opens his mouth to argue. "Please listen to me! You can be mad at me when this over—just go!"

"Oh, I don't think so, my dear." Wind surges around us and lifts Easton at least twenty feet into the air. "As exciting as that was, I find your constant interference tedious. Zeb!" he yells, and a dripping Zeb runs to him. Harrison, slightly singed but otherwise unhurt, flanks my side.

"Charlotte, come here." Hoyt moves in front of us. When Charlotte doesn't immediately move, Easton rises another ten feet. "I hate to repeat myself." Without hesitation, Charlotte runs to his side. He pulls a gun from his side holster and presses it to her temple. "Now, you, brother." Harrison joins them.

"Vivian, I will be taking my brother and my niece. I do hope you will choose to join our cozy reunion. If not, I will no longer consider you an asset but a liability. When I come again it will be to destroy you." His eyes narrow. "What will it be, my dear, your family or your friends?"

"Do you promise to let them go without hurting them?" I ask, not daring to look at Easton.

"Of course." His smile reminds me of a reptile.

"No, V, you can't go with him! You know he's lying!" Abby clings to my arm.

Suddenly, the ground begins to shake and rumble. In unison, everyone, including my uncle, turns toward Ferguson who's once again on his feet and holding his patch in his hand. The quaking grows stronger.

"Ferguson, replace your patch. I have things well in hand." Hoyt struggles to keep his hold on Charlotte and remain standing. Easton yells as he drops rapidly several feet.

With a gasp, I rush forward so that I'm standing beneath him.

"Put him down, Hoyt! You can't hold him like this!" The ground begins to split into tiny cracks.

"Ferguson, stop this shaking now!" Hoyt yells, but Ferguson is clearly beyond orders.

"He killed her!" he shouts. "He killed her, and I'm gonna kill them all!"

"Do something, Zeb!" Hoyt commands. Zeb steps forward, fireball in hand, but Ferguson pinpoints his target through narrowed eyes, and the ground directly beneath him yawns wide. Zeb's screams echo as he tumbles down, lost to the earth beneath.

The ground rumbles its protest, and what began as small cracks around me rapidly become hand-width fissures. Still the shaking continues. Charlotte screams as Hoyt collapses to his knees, dragging her with him. Easton plunges.

"No!" Concentrating all my power on him, I surround him in an orb before he hits the ground.

"Vivian!" Abby yells. The chasm between us is so large Easton and I will have to jump. Taking a few steps back, we race toward the widening space. When my feet hit the other side, the loose dirt gives way and I fall into the gap, gripping the crumbling soil. Easton grabs my hand.

"I've got you!" he yells over the deafening noise as he drags me over.

We crawl over to Cooper, Abby, and the still-unconscious Wyck where they're huddled together on a rapidly shrinking space.

"Harrison!" I yell. He's holding Charlotte tightly, but we're separated by too much space.

"Protect them, Vivian!"

"I can't!" I shake my head, near panic, doubting I'm strong enough to move us all to safety.

"Yes, you can! Concentrate!" He yells back.

Holding out my palm, I close my eyes and imagine an orb glowing brighter than any I've ever created. I see it growing until it closes over us all, above and beneath.

"You did it!" Abby exclaims. I open my eyes to the shimmering ball of energy, and when the ground sinks again, we hover over the top of it. But I won't have the strength to keep it together long. If someone doesn't stop Ferguson, we'll all die very soon.

I hear muffled yells and see the desperation in Harrison's eyes. He's shaking his head and holding onto Hoyt's arm, but Hoyt struggles to stand then holds out both hands, palms facing my father. A powerful wind ripples my light shield and quickly becomes a vortex of swirling nothing, circling my father and Charlotte. They rise off of the ground, suspended as Easton was and protected inside the tornado's center.

Hoyt turns to Ferguson who's remained standing the entire time. Again, I hear their muffled yells then my uncle shifts, his arms spread in a 'T'. The strain shows in his face as he struggles to hold Harrison and Charlotte with one hand. He closes his eyes, and an invisible force blasts toward Ferguson. Ferguson stumbles and drops to one knee, but he raises his head and narrows his eyes. The shaking becomes so bad, trees collapse; the house groans loudly enough to penetrate the orb.

Hoyt, too, falls to his knees, his hands lowering for only a second but long enough that my father and Charlotte nearly touch the ground. He bellows like an angry lion and forces his arm up again. When he closes his eyes this time, the blast is so strong, I see it rip through the air. It smacks Ferguson square in the chest. He flies backward, and the shaking stops abruptly.

Hoyt lowers his hand, and Harrison and Charlotte land gently on the ground, then he falls forward.

Moving us in the shield so that we are above solid ground again, I pull it back inside of me. "Everyone okay?" I ask, looking at each of them.

"I, I think so," Abby says. Cooper and Easton nod. Cooper lays Wyck on the ground and checks Ferguson.

"He's dead."

"Oh, thank, God," Abby sighs.

We carefully pick our way around the split ground toward Harrison and Charlotte. Through tears, Charlotte hugs me while Harrison moves toward his brother's still form. He rolls him onto his back.

"Hoyt!" he exclaims, touching his cheek.

Slowly, Hoyt opens his eyes. But instead of the dead black, they are a vivid moss green. Harrison smiles sadly. "Hello, brother, long time no see."

Hoyt attempts to smile but winces. His body jerks grotesquely.

"What is it?" Harrison asks, running his eyes along Hoyt's body.

"I'm afraid... this... may be our goodbye, brother," he stammers out between whacking breaths.

"What? No! You're a Healer!" Harrison frantically exclaims.

Hoyt's eyes slide momentarily closed. When he opens them again, he looks so tired, old and tired. "Not this time," he whispers. He glances over toward me. "My dear."

I kneel beside him.

"You… must take… care of him… now. He… is… a lot of trouble." He smiles weakly at me, then his brother. "I'm sorry, Harrison."

Harrison kisses Hoyt's forehead. "You were lost."

Hoyt releases a ragged breath. "But… you found me."

"Always, brother." Harrison holds him close to his chest, and Hoyt smiles, exhales, and closes his eyes.

EPILOGUE

"**THIS IS THE LAST ONE.**" I lug the box to the moving truck. My father arranges it inside and pulls down the door. Easton slides the lock into place. Harrison pulls me into a hug, and I smile. I've smiled so much recently, I think I have perma-grin, and that thought makes me smile even more.

"Come on," Charlotte says, holding a bouquet of late-summer wildflowers in her hands.

"One last visit." Wyck drops his arm around Charlotte's shoulders.

All four of us walk into the woods. The boys and my father decided that, just like with Griffin, there might be a lot of questions if we called the police, so they buried Lilah, Ferguson, and Hoyt not far from Griffin. Abby and Cooper had started home the next day, and we've spent the last week packing up what's left of the house.

Charlotte lays the flowers reverently on Hoyt's grave. Wyck takes a couple of sprigs to his brother's grave, and we all stand silently reflecting on all that's happened.

"Is it actually over?" I ask no one in particular.

"Yes, honey, I think it is," Harrison says.

"You really don't think the Liaisons will come looking for them?" Easton asks.

"Oh, they'll look for them, but if I know my brother, they won't find them. He swore he'd never tell where I was hiding."

"It wasn't in any of the records I saw," Wyck says. "I went through everything, and you weren't in there."

"Besides," Charlotte chimes in, "we won't be here anyway." She smiles and hugs Wyck. "I'm excited to start in a real school."

I snort. "Yeah, well, I would hold off on the excitement just yet. What will Trista make of you?" I grin. "I'm glad Abby will have some allies."

"Don't remind me. I can't believe I agreed to this." Wyck rubs his hand over his face, but when Charlotte pokes him in the ribs, he smiles.

"Sure you don't want to join them? We can make that happen," my father asks.

"No way! I'm done with that drama. I'm just fine with my corrupt GED, thank you very much. Easton and I have plans anyway." I squeeze him to me.

He grins roguishly. "Someone's gonna have to keep Cooper and me on track when we get to college."

"Aunt Charlotte would be so happy to know you guys are living in her house."

"*Our* house, honey. You'll be back home occasionally," my father says.

"Oh, I'm sure we will." I sigh watching the sun dip below the trees. "I'm sorry you have to leave all this behind."

"Don't be. It's not going anywhere. We'll be back someday. We should get moving."

"You guys go ahead. I'll be right there." I watch them walk away then I kneel beside my uncle's grave.

It still doesn't seem possible. After all of the running and fighting, it's finally over. We can get on with our lives. And, more unbelievably, we all survived it. What a waste! My uncle, Griffin, even Lilah, Ferguson, and Zeb—wasted Gifts and wasted lives. Hoyt didn't start out evil; his choices turned him that way. I keep picturing that blond boy from the lake who only wanted to take care of the brother he loved.

"Goodbye, Uncle. I'm sorry it had to be this way." And I mean it. I am truly sorry.

"Honey," my father says from close behind me.

I swipe at the lone tear spilling down my cheek. When I stand, he embraces me, giving a lifetime's worth of hugs in that one.

Gazing down at me, he raises his brows. "You ready?"

I smile. "Let's go home, Dad."